The arrival in London of the beautiful 'Mademoiselle Valentine' causes no small stir. But little does Society realise that the dashing young lady masquerading as a French emigrée is really Miss Christy, adventuress.

Her target is the rich and handsome Sir Robert Lyle, whose downfall seems assured until he offers to marry 'Mademoiselle Valentine' and settle her debts. What is Miss Christy to do? To admit her deception is out of the question for there is no one in the world she would rather marry . . .

The Adventuress

Julia Murray

MILLS & BOON LIMITED
London · Sydney · Toronto

First published in Great Britain 1982
by Robert Hale Limited, Clerkenwell House,
Clerkenwell Green, London EC1R 0HT

© Julia Murray 1982

Australian copyright 1983
Philippine copyright 1983

This edition published 1983
by Mills & Boon Limited, 15–16 Brook's Mews,
London W1A 1DR

ISBN 0 263 74458 2

Set in 10 on 11½ pt Linotron Times
04/1183

Photoset by Rowland Phototypesetting Ltd
Bury St Edmunds, Suffolk
Made and printed in Great Britain by
Cox & Wyman Ltd, Reading

CHAPTER
ONE

HE was a tall, dark man with powerful chest and shoulders. In repose his face was harsh, the line of his jaw firm, the mouth a hard unyielding line. When he smiled a warmth lit his face, investing those dark, almost black eyes with a wicked charm that had melted many a foolish heart. He wore his clothes with a negligence many a man would consider shameful, and no one could doubt the rumour that little more than a quarter of an hour was ever wasted upon his neckcloth. His coats might be made by the best tailors, Weston, perhaps, or Schultz, and pressed by a first-class valet; no wrinkle ever marred their perfection, it was true, but somehow they never managed to look quite the thing on those powerful shoulders or when buttoned across that broad chest. Yet Sir Robert's friends valued his companionship, and many a lady, though she kept her daughters well out of his way, had been known to follow him with her eyes as he crossed a crowded room.

Sir Robert Lyle, apparently little the worse for drink, watched expressionlessly as across the table his handsome young half-brother pushed a pile of rouleaus towards the Bank. Joseph, while drinking rather more heavily than his brother, was not yet in his cups, and Sir Robert allowed reluctantly that at least the fellow did not frequently end beneath the table. His eye might sparkle, and the arrangement of his cravat was not the perfect Waterfall it had once been, but he was still a stylish young gentleman, his hair arranged to a nicety à la Brutus, his coat of olive superfine sitting with perfection across his shoulders. Made by Schultz, Sir Robert suspected, his lip curling slightly.

Joseph had been betting recklessly, and it was Sir Robert's opinion that he would, by morning, be required to redeem those carelessly scribbled vowels, or see his brother in Newgate. He sighed, and signalled to the lackey to refill his glass. Had he known Joseph intended visiting this select little establishment he would have avoided it. Now he was obliged to witness his brother gamble away the better part of five hundred pounds.

Sir Robert was a modest winner. Faro was not a game he favoured, preferring to chance his hand with the cards, but the smile and nod of a friend had drawn him and he had not played at piquet. When Joseph arrived he had not noticed his elder brother at first, or almost certainly he would have shunned the table, but by the time that harsh dark face had drawn his attention he had already suffered his first loss. A frown flickered across the handsome face, and then he smiled, and bowed.

'Good evening, Robert. I had not known you intended to be here.' He spoke pleasantly, but there was a wariness in the grey eyes.

'Nor I you,' Sir Robert returned, pushing his wager across the table. 'Your dear mother, she is well?'

'Thank you, yes.' Joseph spoke shortly, his attention being claimed by the progress of the game.

They did not speak again, Joseph being more concerned with his losses, and Sir Robert growing more and more grim as he watched the rouleaus exchange hands.

Joseph was a fool. Sir Robert had always known it, but never before had he been privileged to witness his stupidity at a gaming-table. He had known about it well enough; only too often had he been called upon to settle his mammoth debts, not only to his friends but to tradesmen all over London. Had peace with France not been signed the year before he might have considered the purchase of a pair of colours for the young man. As it was, two months previously he had given Joseph a strict injunction to keep within his allowance, since when he had not seen his brother. He had been hoping he had mended his ways: tonight had shown him the folly of such expectation.

At about two o'clock he rose from the table and gathered his winnings. Opposite him Joseph was scribbling another vowel, but as the movement caught his eye he looked up. In a moment he, too, had risen from the table, but with a request that his place be kept for him.

'I was wanting to speak with you, Robert. I'm glad you're here.'

They were in the vestibule, and the lackey was handing Sir Robert his hat and cane. 'I am leaving now; if you want to talk you had better walk with me.'

For a moment Joseph frowned, and then he nodded. He was not wishful to argue with his brother just now. They left the club together.

The night air was chill and the street deserted. Joseph turned up the collar of his cloak. 'I'm glad to see you, Robert,' he began, as his brother strode away down the street. 'There is something of a particular nature I wish to ask you.'

'If it is for an increase in your allowance you're wasting your time,' Sir Robert answered shortly.

'No,' Joseph replied, although he was desperately

short of funds, 'it's about Great-uncle Claudius. My mother's had the most extraordinary letter.'

'She has?'

Sir Robert's interest was minimal, but Joseph refused to be dismayed. 'Yes. It is the most awkward thing. Indeed, I can hardly credit it.' He glanced at his brother, but there was no sign that he even heard. 'He is to be married, to some wench a quarter his age. Mama is furious.'

'I fail to see that it is any concern of your mother's,' Sir Robert remarked.

Joseph controlled his impatience with difficulty. 'I dare say it means nothing to you, why should it? But I am Claudius's heir!'

'I had not forgotten.'

'If he marries,' Joseph persisted, 'I shall be quite done up. If he does not father a whelp, he'll probably leave her all his blunt, and then I shall be in the devil's own fix.'

'I don't see what you can hope to do about it, Joseph. If the girl is so young there is very little chance of your outliving her.'

'Don't provoke me, Robert,' Joseph said, laying one hand on his brother's arm. 'I warn you, this affair is close to my heart.'

Sir Robert turned, and gently removed Joseph's hand. 'You rumple my sleeve,' he said.

With an effort Joseph controlled himself. 'Will you help me, or not? He would listen to you. Go to Bedfordshire, talk some sense into the old gentleman. Lord, Robert, is it so very much to ask?'

'It is a great deal too much,' Sir Robert responded coldly, turning and walking on. 'Ask your mother.'

'You know he cannot abide her,' Joseph exclaimed, hurrying to catch him up. 'I dare say she would have gone, had she thought it would do the least particle of good, but he will not even let her in the house.'

'Which I can only consider a piece of very good sense,' Sir Robert returned irritatingly. He reached the steps to his house and stopped. 'Do not think, Joseph, that you can bring your losses to me in the morning. I have no intention, as I told you before, of settling any more of your debts. Goodnight to you.'

'You won't go to Bedfordshire?'

'Goodnight, Joseph.'

For a moment the young man stood staring at the door as it closed behind Sir Robert, then he turned on his heel and made his way back to the club.

Sir Robert, who had always intended travelling into Bedfordshire, was on the road while his brother yet lay abed. His great-uncle's betrothal had been announced to him some three days previously, in a letter, and he had always assumed that his stepmother Lavinia, Lady Lyle, would have received a similar missive. He had no intention of persuading the old gentleman to abandon the match; if he chose, at the age of seventy, to attach himself to some wench Sir Robert could only wish him well. He merely wanted to assure himself that his favourite relative was not being grossly taken-in.

Sir Robert had so far eschewed the married state. He had seen not the slightest need to burden himself with a woman, and now, at thirty-seven, it was beginning to seem more and more likely that he would never find that need. Being possessed of a certain charm, although his harsh features lacked his half-brother's obvious good looks, his smile and his substantial fortune ensured the willingness of almost any pretty face his fancy might light upon. Since it rarely lit upon any of the more acceptable ladies of his acquaintance, but usually those who were married already, there had never been the least need for him to tread the path to the altar, and if he were quickly establishing for himself the reputation of a rake he was the least concerned. Only the most ambitious, or most desperate, mother would throw her daughter in his path now; he was destined, it seemed, to enjoy a far greater freedom than anyone would have thought possible when he had come upon the Town, his money and rank newly acquired, some sixteen years before.

His manner of travelling to Bedfordshire was quite typical of him. He drove himself in his curricle, his tiger clinging perilously to his perch in the rear as the sporting vehicle hurtled its way northwards. Always impatient Sir Robert drove today as though a demon were behind him, stopping only to effect the necessary changes. Since he had made an early start he was in Bedfordshire in time for dinner, knowing that in spite of the fact he was not expected he would find himself more than welcome. His Great-uncle Claudius had never had a love of husbandry, and it would seem as though little had changed, or indeed would change with his forthcoming marriage. The curricle rattled and swayed over the ruts of the drive, its wheels periodically dropping into the potholes and threatening to deposit driver and tiger together among the bushes. They arrived safely, however, before the stately Georgian mansion, the lights blazing in several downstairs apartments telling them that the master was indeed at home. Before the curricle had come fully to rest the tiger had sprung from his perch, and now, as Sir Robert dropped to the ground, had taken control of the horses. Sir Robert gave him a careless nod, and proceeded to the front door.

He had expected his arrival to be remarked, but when having beaten a sharp tattoo upon the brass knocker no one came in answer to his summons he sighed and pushed open the door. It was plain his arrival had not been remarked. Indeed, as he stood in the open doorway, he began to wonder just what he would need to do to attract someone's attention. The house was plainly occupied, for sounds of considerable anger were emanating from a chamber to his right. Sir Robert entered the hall, and closed the door behind him. At that moment a man appeared, withdrawing from the room in which the old man clearly was, bowing agitatedly and assuring the unseen gentleman that it would be attended to at once. With a sigh the harassed individual shut the door and turned, and only then espied the late arrival.

'Why, Sir Robert!' he exclaimed, one hand going automatically to his ordered neckcloth. 'I must beg your pardon. I was not apprised of your arrival.'

'It is of no moment, Chivers,' Sir Robert assured him. 'My uncle, it would seem, is a trifle distressed.'

'Yes, sir, indeed, sir. In fact, sir, I believe it is a great piece of good fortune that you have arrived, if you will forgive my boldness. It is possible, sir, that you might be able to do something.'

Sir Robert controlled his features. 'Whatever has occurred?' he inquired solicitously, inwardly cursing an absurd desire to laugh. 'Your master is not ill?'

The butler shook his head. 'No, sir, but I must admit that I have rarely seen him so agitated.' He glanced fleetingly over his shoulder and then added in a hushed voice, 'It's the young lady.'

'Indeed!'

'Yes, sir. Miss Grant. I should tell you sir, that my master has lately entered upon an Engagement.'

'Yes, Chivers, I did know.'

'Yes, sir. Well, as I say, it is Miss Grant. It would seem, sir, as though she has departed.'

'Departed?'

'Yes, sir. She was to have dined, you understand, but she has just now sent word that she cannot come. She has seen fit, sir, to terminate the engagement.'

'Indeed, Chivers.'

'Yes, sir. I tell you this, sir, I hope you understand, that you might be able to assist my master in his trouble. He is quite likely, I believe, to order you from the house.'

Sir Robert repressed a smile. 'He is?'

'Yes, sir. It would seem, sir, as though the young lady has—er—possessed herself of quite a considerable amount of my master's money, not stolen, you understand, but borrowed. It is that, I believe, that has made my master so *particularly* angry. In fact, sir, he had instructed me to summon Sir Josiah, the magistrate.'

'Indeed!' Sir Robert's amusement was but barely concealed. 'I wish you might not do that, Chivers, until I have had a chance to speak with my uncle.'

'Well, sir, I—'

'Chivers, please do as I bid. I feel there is more to this than is immediately apparent, and I should appreciate the opportunity for a little conversation alone with your master.'

'Very good, sir,' Chivers said, more than a little relieved to have passed the responsibility on to such patently capable shoulders. He waited until he had seen Sir Robert enter the dining-room, and then, in anticipation of an explosion, hurriedly made his escape to the servants' hall.

CHAPTER
TWO

Miss Genevieve Christy's horses had made good speed:
they reached Luton before eight o'clock that night. The
best inn in that small town was the George, but Miss
Christy, suddenly cautious, had ordered the coachman
to carry her to the Angel, a far less prepossessing
hostelry some distance from the main street. The young
gentleman escorting her on horseback had protested
somewhat volubly at this sudden departure, but to no
avail. They were by no means far enough away, she told
him, to be putting up in the first hotels. He continued to
grumble, however, particularly when the dinner they
were served proved to be neither of the finest nor
particularly hot, but Miss Christy seemed not to care,
and indeed, took no notice.

Their arrival had produced something of a stir among
the staff at the Angel Inn. The sight of a carriage, hired,
it was true, but with four steaming horses, drawing up in
the modest yard had sent Mr Briggs hurrying into the
kitchens. He had bidden reluctant kitchen-maid and
cook bestir themselves if they were able, for he knew
Quality when he saw it, and it was up to them to make
the best of it. He had then taken himself upstairs to the
hall, where he had bowed the young couple in, certain
now that his instincts had been quite correct. Weary and
travel-stained they might be, but Mr Briggs' keen eye

was yet able to detect the excellence of the young gentleman's many-caped great-coat, and the quality of his hessians, generously covered in mud though they were. The young lady, moreover, proved to be such an exquisite picture of loveliness that the unfortunate Mr Briggs was betrayed into staring, a fact which was pointed out to him by the young gentleman, in a manner far from patient. Mr Briggs apologised profusely, but indeed, he was to be forgiven, for Miss Christy, in spite of the exigencies of her journey, did look particularly fine. The yellow curls framing a perfect oval face set with the most enormous blue eyes Mr Briggs had ever seen, and topped by a bonnet with a very high poke, were designed to captivate, and captivate they did. Mr Briggs might have been quite unaware that the blue of Miss Christy's modish pelisse was almost exactly the blue of her eyes, which was the reason for their appearance of outstanding colour, but he was perfectly aware of the smile with which she favoured him as she asked if he had two bedchambers to spare, together with a private room, and a bed for her maid. He was happy to inform them, he said, that he did have just such rooms available at the present time, but only due to a sudden cancellation, otherwise he would almost certainly have been unable to oblige. Miss Christy smiled again and thanked him, asking if she might see her chamber immediately as she was anxious to put off her pelisse.

Mr George Christy, the dapper young gentleman aforementioned, continued throughout the evening to complain. His room was too small, his bed too hard, and the mug of ale with which he had been served in the tap-room too abominable to drink. He had been obliged to arrange his neckcloth by the light of a single branch of candles, and though he had wasted nearly an hour upon it, as his sister well knew, he doubted that the effect was at all what he desired. 'It is a Mailcoach,' he explained, 'and you know how difficult *that* is. Yet when I summoned the maid to request another branch she told me I had all that there were, in the most insolent manner imaginable.'

For as long as she was able his sister bore this in silence, but she was finally driven to expostulation, and expressed a wish that he might just hold his tongue, as she now had the headache.

'Well,' exclaimed the young exquisite, 'if that don't just take the biscuit! What about me, eh? You don't have to sleep upon a bed as hard as a board and pull off your boots with a jack, which I have had to do, let me tell you. And I dare say the marks will never be removed, not if Collins should polish them in champagne for a month.'

Miss Christy did not reply.

'Why we couldn't bring him this time I don't know,' the young man continued peevishly, plucking at his sleeve with an irritated gesture. 'You always take Mary with you. Chances are by the time we get to London someone will have stolen him from me!'

'You know that is hardly likely,' Miss Christy remarked, attempting to be patient. 'I dare say no one was ever more faithful than Collins. And don't forget it is Mary we have to thank for that.'

'Stupid abigail!' muttered the young man, a frown creasing the smooth perfection of his youthful brow.

His sister smiled, fleetingly. 'You would not call her so, you well know, if she were only young and pretty. I dare say you'd only be too glad to have her with us all the time.'

'Aye, so I should!' young Christy exclaimed, scraping

back his chair and standing up. 'I'm heartily sick, let me tell you, of staying in the background, and if you think I'm going to do that in London, well, all I can say is, you're mightily mistaken.'

'I have been thinking about that,' Miss Christy remarked, frowning a little. 'It might be better, after all, if you were to set up on your own for a while. It will be much easier for me, you know, if no one knows exactly who you are.'

'Run my own rig, you mean? Would you trust me?'

The young woman smiled. 'I don't know. Should I?'

'I wish you would!' he exclaimed, all signs of irritation suddenly gone. 'I dare say I am quite capable now of taking care of myself. In fact,' he continued gravely, 'I have been wondering whether I should let you run another rig so soon. There is no saying but what someone might recognise you one day.'

'They might,' she conceded, 'but it's unlikely, and besides, I have been very careful. Claudius Lyle never leaves his mansion, you should know that; the chances are I shall be perfectly safe, and besides, I shall not be Miss Persephone Grant any longer.'

'Of course not, but who will you be?'

She smiled mischievously. '*Eh bien, chéri*, per'aps ze French *émigrée, oui*? What say you?'

'Perfect! You know, Gen, you're a trump, you really are! But shall you be able to carry it off? What if someone should question you?'

She contemplated him from beneath long dark lashes. 'Do you doubt me? I have no fear but that Mlle Valentine Deneuve will be all the rage in London, and within a very short space of time.'

The young man smiled. 'Very well. One last rig. A big one.'

She nodded, 'Indeed. This time I shall make sure it is a very large fish indeed.'

One particularly large fish, having partaken of an excellent, if hasty, dinner in Bedfordshire, was at that moment seated in his curricle, his high-crowned beaver pushed firmly onto his dark locks, his many-caped driving-coat ballooning out behind him with the speed of his progress. He had found his great-uncle in a state of some distress. Whatever surprise the old man might have felt at his great-nephew's sudden and unexpected appearance was rapidly overcome by the extent of his wrath, and after telling the gentleman pithily that if he meant to gloat he could take himself off, had handed him a sheet of hot-pressed paper and sunk into a chair.

The letter was short, and to the point. Miss Grant had apparently thought better of her engagement to Mr Claudius Lyle and so, out of deference to his feelings and a wish not to cause either of them pain, she was removing herself at once from his vicinity. His expression unusually grim Sir Rober had turned to his great-uncle and asked one short question. The old man let out a roar.

'Yes, I gave her money. It's obvious, ain't it? Been had for a fool, at my age! You'll tell me I should have known better, but if you do, Robert, you can leave my house this minute.'

'No, uncle, I'll not say that, but I shall leave, as soon as I've had something to eat. I'd go now, but I've not eaten all day.'

'Devil take you, Robert, you don't think I meant it, do you? Damme, I've got enough to tackle without you getting on your high horse!'

Sir Robert smiled. 'I'd not take offence at anything you could say, you should know that. But I had a mind to meet Miss Grant, and that had not abated. In fact, my desire is keener than ever.'

The old man regarded him from beneath shaggy brows. 'You'll bring her back?'

He nodded. 'I've no mind to see her get away with this; forgive me, but I doubt if this is the first time.'

'Devil a bit!' growled the old man, his white brows bristling. 'Spun me such a yarn, too! Some flash cove dunning her for money, and I believed her!'

'To what extent? How much did you give her?'

'Two thousand, burn it! Had for a fool! You bring her back, Robert, and I'll not forget it. If only I hadn't sent that accursed letter! Lavinia will be quite puffed up, I make no doubt!'

'You'll marry her if I bring her back?' Sir Robert could not resist asking.

'Devil a bit! I want my money, and there's an end to it! I had in mind to send for Sir Josiah, the Justice, but I shall need to think about that. Just bring her back, Robert, that's all I ask, and say nothing to that pea-goose.'

Sir Robert nodded. 'Very well. But shall we dine? She has a fair start over me already.'

'Humph. They'll tell you at the inn, no doubt, which road she took. Just mind you don't break your stupid neck in that dashed foolish vehicle of yours.'

For a while it looked as though Sir Robert were determined to disobey his great-uncle's last wish. Shortly after they had passed through Streatley it started to rain, but he slackened his pace not one jot: indeed, his tiger even thought he increased it. Miss Grant, it seemed, had taken the London road; he knew what time she had departed, it was in his mind that she must stop at Luton that night, and he intended being there before she left again in the morning. Travelling through the evening he pulled up in the yard of the George Inn shortly before eleven, but, to his dismay, no carriage or person answering to Miss Grant's description had stopped there that evening. For a moment he hesitated, unable to decide whether to put up there anyway or proceed to St Albans. As he pondered the ostler cleared his throat and ventured the information that there was another hostelry, but that he had hesitated to mention it as it was hardly suited to the gentleman's standing.

Sir Robert fixed him with a steely eye. 'Where, man? Tell me!'

'The Angel, sir, next to the church.' He gestured vaguely and added, 'You can't miss it.'

Sir Robert nodded curtly. With a jerk of his head he indicated to his tiger to be mounted, and then, with a sparking of hooves on the cobbles, they lurched out into the street again. It was dark, but Sir Robert found the church, with the Angel Inn at its side. By this time he was so weary he would have put up in a barn, so it was fortunate that the overawed boy who ran out to attend to him was able to give the answer he desired. The lady was putting up at the Angel, indeed, together with her brother and her abigail.

'Good. Stable my horses. I shall require chambers for myself and a bed for my tiger.'

He swung himself down on the words and entered the dismal hostelry, anxious now only for a glass of brandy and a bed to himself. The landlord came bowing, and acceded to his request. He had a chamber, he said, but only on account of a sudden cancellation, otherwise he would almost certainly have been full. The private room, however, had been taken these two hours by a young lady and her brother.

'It is of no consequence,' Sir Robert replied, 'as I shall not be here above a night. You may tell me, however, who is the young lady. It is possible I may be acquainted with her.'

'A Miss Christy, sir, a most charming young woman, if I may be permitted to say so.'

'Hmm. I don't know her.' He smiled at the landlord. 'Handsome, is she?'

'A picture, sir, a veritable picture.'

Sir Robert nodded and smiled again. 'In that case I must hope to be meeting Miss Christy in Town. I am journeying there myself.'

'Then most certainly you will, for I heard her say that she hoped they would be in London on the morrow.'

'Then if you would show me my room I shall retire,' Sir Robert said, turning towards the stairs. 'I must needs make an early start, and have been travelling nearly all day.'

It was at this point that a door opened at the far end of the dismal hall and a young lady, deep in conversation with a smart young buck in olive superfine, stepped into the passage and headed for the the stairs. To allow her to pass Sir Robert stood back a pace and bowed, but she barely glanced at him or even seemed to realise he was there. Sir Robert was amused, and not ungrateful. It was unlikely, he thought, that she would ever recognise him again. In the meantime, he had had plentiful opportunity to observe the cause of his great-uncle's downfall, and to allow that at least he could not fault the old man's taste. The wench was certainly a beauty, even if his own inclination was not for blondes, and he had no doubt but that she would find herself an instant success in London. Following her with his eyes as she mounted the stairs he had an excellent opportunity to observe the elegance of a particularly well-turned ankle, and the way, if he had chosen, her blue eyes sparkled when she was animated. He turned back to the landlord with a twinkle in his own dark eyes, but all he said was, 'Please be good enough to show me to my room. I am much fatigued.'

The landlord bowed. Sir Robert was conducted to his chamber, a small but sufficient room, where he closeted himself with a bottle of brandy and his thoughts, pulling off his own boots with a jack, and with very little concern for the welfare of the leather.

He was downstairs betimes the following morning, having performed his own toilet with a haste many would have been appalled at, and which would have cast his worthy valet into a fit of the dismals had he been permitted to see how little he was needed. Descending to the breakfast parlour Sir Robert ascertained that he was ahead of Miss Christy, but even as he sat he heard footsteps on the stairs, and in a moment the door to the private room open and close. He was not permitted another view of the young lady, but this did not grieve him, and he was out of the hotel and into his curricle well before Miss Christy was prepared to leave. Under the cover of discussion with his tiger he watched as her carriage was prepared for a journey, a large quantity of baggage being strapped to the roof and cast into the capacious boot. As he delayed a young man, the same he had observed the night before, appeared from the hotel and mounted onto the back of a showy horse, and Sir Robert deduced that the journey was about to commerce. He allowed her a fair start. It would gall him, he well knew, to travel at the pace of a hired carriage, but he had no option, since it was his desire to know exactly where Miss Christy intended to lodge once resident in the Metropolis. To his tiger's amazement, therefore, they completed the journey at an uncharacteristically leisurely pace, the carriage sometimes in sight, but usually not, until they came into the suburbs of London. Now Sir Robert drew up close. There was little chance, he well knew, of his being recognised, and nothing would be easier than to lose the young lady in the crush of a busy afternoon. He noticed grimly that she appeared to know exactly where she was going, and as the carriage pulled up outside the Pulteney Hotel he found himself wondering just how much of his uncle's money she would be obliged to spend to keep herself there. Having seen her safely installed he whipped up his horses again and proceeded to his house in Berkeley Square, to discover that his unfortunate valet had departed for Bedfordshire earlier that day.

CHAPTER
THREE

THE Honourable Miss Selina Pinkerton had taken herself to Grafton House unbeknownst to her maid, and was hoping that no one she knew would see her there. She was a tall woman, slightly too tall, perhaps, of just turned forty, with an infallible eye for the becoming. Her lack of funds had not prevented her from donning that morning a shallow-crowned bonnet with a modest poke that set off to admiration her long, kind face with its grey eyes and generous mouth, a bonnet that had performed the same office for the past five seasons at least, trimmed by ribbons of different hues. Economy had long since been of prime importance to her, and it was some little while, now, since she had discovered that one could purchase certain items at Grafton House for a fraction of the cost elsewhere. Of course, one was obliged to rub shoulders with the hoy-poloy, which she still did with great unwillingness, but the muslins were really so cheap, as were the silk stockings, that indeed it was quite worth the inconvenience. As usual the place was almost unbearably crowded, and the salesgirls were really quite insolent, speaking to one as though one were quite the dregs of society, instead of the daughter of an earl and a member of one of the oldest houses in the country. Nevertheless Miss Pinkerton went about her business with a will, selecting muslins and lace handkerchiefs, and discovering to her joy a quite fine zephyr shawl almost tossed to one side by the fat woman in front of her. It was as she pored over this trophy exulting in the knowledge that it would be perfect for her niece's début and would save her spending anywhere near the amount that might otherwise have been necessary, that she heard a distinctly French voice at her elbow, youthful and particularly charming. She turned her head.

'*Pardonez moi*,' the voice continued, 'but I wonder, are you purchasing the shawl?'

For a moment the good woman frowned. Before her stood a young woman of unquestionable beauty, but for a moment her standing eluded her. To be sure, she was dressed in the height of fashion; even Miss Pinkerton's experienced eye could detect no fault with the sable-trimmed pelisse and matching blue kid gloves, or the bonnet with very high poke that framed such a perfectly oval face. It was merely her presence here in this emporium of the lower classes that threw the good lady for a brief moment. Then she smiled. The girl was French, of course. 'I believe I am,' she answered firmly, but investing her voice with a touch of kindness. The girl was quite lovely, after all.

'*Eh bien*, forgive me, madame. It is just that I search for such a shawl for my evening gown, you understand. Pray excuse.'

The girl bowed her head with great formality and would have withdrawn had not Miss Pinkerton, loath, for some curious reason, to let the beauty slip away, said quickly, 'Forgive me, but are you not French?'

The girl beamed and nodded. 'Indeed, madame! 'Ow clever of you to notice! My accent, it is very bad, no?'

'Quite charming,' Miss Pinkerton told her truthfully.

'Permit me to introduce myself. Selina Pinkerton, my dear.'

''Ow do you do,' the young lady said, holding out one gloved hand. 'I am Mademoiselle Valentine Deneuve, and I 'ave, as you understand, but lately journeyed from France.'

'Ah,' breathed Miss Pinkerton comprehending, 'you are an émigrée!'

The girl nodded delightedly. 'Assuredly. 'Ow very clever of you!'

'Not at all. Tell me, where are you staying?'

'At the—er—Pulteney, madame. You know it?'

'Most certainly. Tell me, my dear, do you know many people in London? I don't believe we have met before, at any function?'

The girl shook her head. 'Truly, madame, I know no one! It 'as been a cause of the great distress to me! My parents, they are dead, and in England I know no one. It is very 'ard.'

'It must be quite terrible,' Miss Pinkerton agreed, frowning slightly. 'Tell me, are you nearly finished here? I have just these few purchases to make and then I shall be returning home. I wish you would come and take tea with me!'

The girl smiled shyly. 'Madame, truly, that is very kind of you!'

'Good. If you would just wait a moment or two while I catch a girl—ah good.' Having succeeded in waylaying a harassed salesgirl Miss Pinkerton completed her transaction and was free in a very few minutes to conduct the Mademoiselle Deneuve and her maid out to her waiting carriage.

Miss Christy, having dismissed her sour-faced maid with a flow of rapid French of which Miss Pinkerton understood very little, climbed into the slightly shabby vehicle that awaited them and seated herself, prepared to be delighted with everything she should see. Having started to regret her new acquaintance—the carriage, after all, did not speak the wealth she had hoped for— the young woman was delighted to notice the direction they took, and when they came to a halt outside a tall house in Brunswick Square congratulated herself that her instinct had not failed her yet. Even when it transpired that Miss Pinkerton occupied a mere one floor of the elegant house her good humour did not abate, for she saw clearly that Miss Pinkerton, while not wealthy, as she had hoped, might yet be able to perform those introductions she wished for, and chaperon her into society.

For her part, Miss Pinkerton found her new friend to be quite delightful. She was everything that was proper—beautiful, of course, but with such a becoming deference about her, and that charming accent—The good lady, who lived alone, began to conceive of a plan, she must have considered extraordinary a day before, and as she watched the animated face before her decided that she might find it quite enjoyable. One was so lonely these days, it had to be admitted. Of course, she had her nephews and nieces, charming every one, but with their own lives now and very little time to spare for a spinster aunt who lived in such a modest way. There was Henry, of course, her brother, to whom she owed the extremely pleasant apartment she now occupied, but he was becoming such a bore these days, talking of nothing but his horses, besides being so grossly fat she did not quite like to be seen with him. The more she considered it the more it seemed as though her chance encounter might provide her with a little harmless pleasure, besides doing

someone a very valuable service indeed. For some
little time, until after her thirtieth birthday in fact, Miss
Pinkerton had continued to hope that luck would throw
in her way a gentleman to whom the lack of fortune
would be quite immaterial. In her youth, she had not
been unhandsome, but what bloom she had had faded
early, and now, at forty, she looked precisely what she
was, a lonely spinster, with very little else to think about
but how to make last year's gown tolerable again for the
new season, and whether or not she could persuade
Milly to use tallow candles occasionally instead of the
expensive wax. Henry would have helped her, she knew,
for Henry had married Money, even if it did have its
origins in the City and ought therefore to be despised.
But she had never liked taking charity, and had she not
been quite homeless would not even have accepted his
offer of a roof. She had never had cause to regret this,
however. Of course, she might have moved out to
Kensington, or Wimbledon, or some such place, but she
would have been so lonely, and bored, quite separated
from all she loved and that was familiar to her. Her
apartment was small, but so cosy, so convenient, and she
had about her those things of her own that made life
tolerable, things like her mother's old chiffonier and
Papa's old armchair, neither of which Henry had wanted
and which he would probably have burned. The more
she watched the girl opposite her the more the idea of
chaperoning her into society grew. It would be like
having a daughter of one's own, wouldn't it? Something
she had always wanted.

Quite aware that her hostess, in spite of her nods and
smiles, was not listening to a single word she said Miss
Christy chattered on, inventing her life history as she
talked, discovering inconsistencies and removing them

as she might not otherwise have done. By the time Miss Pinkerton became attentive again she had reached England, with her maid and her belongings, only to discover that the friend of her mother with whom she was to live had died but the week before. This last fact Miss Pinkerton fully assimilated, and frowned a little.

'Forgive me, my dear, but do you have any money? You are staying at the Pulteney, after all, which is not inexpensive. Quite the contrary, in fact!'

'Yes, madame, I know. It is only until I find somewhere else. *Mon père*, my father, you understand, was used to speak of it, so when I came to London I asked that the coachman should take me there. After I arrived, only, I realise it is expense.'

'Expensive,' Miss Pinkerton corrected her absently. An even yet more daring scheme had entered her brain. Was she quite mad? Or just growing old and foolish? She decided she was neither, and smiled upon the young woman. She was little more than a child, after all—what harm could there possibly be?

Miss Christy took up residence with her maid within the week. She had tried, at first, although with little reluctance, to refuse the good lady's offer, but to no avail. Miss Pinkerton, having once decided, would not be put off, and could only regard the child's reluctance to disturb her as very pretty and becoming. So she was ensconced in a room of her own, not large, but sufficient for her needs, which, she insisted, were utterly modest. And from the first it seemed to Miss Pinkerton as though nothing could be more delightful. The child was a perfect dream, charming to have near one, ever helpful, and even willing, Miss Pinkerton soon discovered, to attend to the most idle chatter. She had clothes aplenty, it seemed, but they nevertheless revelled in visiting the shops together and buying silly trifles, such as the perfectly delightful chip-straw bonnet that looked utterly charming on top of Mademoiselle's yellow curls, and would not withstand the slightest breeze or drop of moisture. There was a parasol, too, such as Miss Pinkerton had hankered after but had never dared buy for herself, but which looked so right with the hat, and the primrose kid gloves that went with nothing at all. Miss Pinkerton had long since parted with the zephyr shawl that had brought them together, for indeed it had looked utterly right with Mademoiselle's evening gown, and was now, albeit half-heartedly, searching for something to give her niece. And wherever they went Miss Pinkerton introduced her to her friends, to her acquaintances, and to people she usually only nodded at in passing. One and all had seemed charmed by her protégée, as she had known they would, and very shortly the invitations began to arrive. Mademoiselle seemed quite overwhelmed by it all, and was continually expressing her thanks, until she realised that her hostess was deriving quite as much pleasure as she, and really did not want to be thanked at all. So she kissed her faded cheek and left it at that, ensuring that the unfortunate woman was more entranced than ever.

Only Henry seemed unaffected by her charm. The Earl of Maland, discovering quite by chance that his usually sober sister had apparently run quite mad and was escorting all over town a wench of whom nobody knew anything at all, had arrived one morning in Brunswick Square, anxious to see for himself just what maggot had got into Selina's brain. He had soon discovered, and had not liked it at all. To be sure, Mlle Deneuve had put herself out to be charming, but since the gentleman was not prepared to be charmed that day, having had crab

the night before which now appeared to be disagreeing
with him, she found her attempts to be wasted. His
lordship was utterly suspicious, it was quite plain, and
when he requested that she leave the room so he might
discuss some business with his sister, Miss Christy had
known some quite severe misgivings. It would be too
much to bear if all her hard work were to be undone
now, just when she seemed to be getting what she
wanted. She had done her best to listen at the door, but
the appearance of Milly, Miss Pinkerton's maid, had
forced her to go away, and pass the next half-hour in a
fever of anxiety in her own room. But she need not have
worried. Miss Pinkerton was quite equal to an argument
with her brother, for indeed she had expected it, since
nothing was more likely than that Henry would try to
throw a spoke in her wheel. He had three daughters of
his own to establish, after all, and every one of them was
as plain as a pikestaff, even Jane, her own favourite, who
had once been destined to receive the zephyr shawl. Of
course, Henry would try to knock the thing on the head,
Miss Pinkerton had known that from the start, and had
steeled herself to take absolutely no notice of anything
he might say. So, while the Earl departed confident that
he had managed to instil some sense into his sister, Miss
Pinkerton was even then planning what the child should
wear to her first soirée, and wondering whether her own
diamonds, left to her by her mother, would appear too
heavy against the girl's slender neck.

Sir Robert received the news of Miss Christy's remov-
al with a curl of his thin lip. He had to admire the young
woman as a clever and rapid worker. Since her design
must be to get herself accepted into society she could
hardly have done better, for Miss Pinkerton, although
indeed not wealthy, was a woman of unimpeachable

birth and background, the perfect person to give her credence.

He was not permitted to witness Mlle Deneuve's eruption into society for he did not attend the soirée in question, but he heard about it, and what he heard made him smile in appreciation. It had been a small affair, which was a pity, he thought, since the young woman was surely worthy of a much wider audience. Nevertheless it appeared as though she had done her best, for those gentlemen who had been privileged to meet her proved unable to speak of anything else on the following morning. Had Sir Robert not possessed such an interest he must have been most heartily bored. As it was, he resolved to get himself invited, at whatever cost, to the next function at which he might reasonably expect to meet Mlle Deneuve.

He was granted the opportunity within a very few days. The beginning of the season was almost with them; already hostesses were planning their balls and entertainments, each determined that hers, above all others, should be remembered as the event of the year. Despite his slightly unsavoury reputation Sir Robert Lyle usually found himself with more invitations than he cared for, and it had seemed to him, in the past, that the pre-season entertainments were getting earlier and earlier. This year, however, the ball at the Delaney's, so early as to be almost ridiculous, seemed likely to be the answer to all his wishes. Mrs Delaney was launching yet another of her gawky daughters; the early début was, no doubt, an attempt on the part of a desperate woman to steal a march over the undoubted beauties that would be appearing later in the season. To be sure, many families had yet to return from the country, a factor the good lady had considered most carefully, but to be weighed against

this was the indisputable fact that her poor Eliza, dear
child though she certainly was, would be unable to hold a
candle to the more accredited beauties, and would have
to take the best she could get. She had regarded it as a
most unwelcome thing that her dear friend and bosom-
bow, Selina Pinkerton, should choose just now for her
extraordinary venture, and since she had been permitted
to meet Mlle Deneuve one morning in the park she could
only think it a stroke of most ill-luck. Selina could not be
denied, of course, and besides, the foreign creature was
such a paragon she would probably be engaged before
the season was properly begun.

Sir Robert Lyle prepared himself for the evening with
his customary carelessness. His valet having finally returned from Bedfordshire Sir Robert was obliged to
suffer the good fellow's ministrations, and departed for
his ball, therefore, rather more elegantly attired than
might otherwise have been possible. His valet's concern
for his own reputation rather than his master's had much
to do with the impeccable small-clothes and black satin
knee-breeches, but it was his own taste that led him to
arrange the exquisitely starched cravat within a very few
minutes indeed, favouring none of the more extravagant
styles that characterised the dandies of the day. Denby
might shudder to see the pristine cloth so maltreated but
Sir Robert did not, and indeed, having selected at
random a single fob, departed for the evening feeling
nothing more than a dashed dandy himself. However
that might have been, his hostess, at least, was extremely
gratified to see so valued a guest make such an effort for
her daughter and resolved, as she watched him tread up
her wide stairway, that in spite of his shocking reputation he should have one dance, at least, with her dearest
child.

Sir Robert entered the extensive ballroom with a feeling of great misgiving. His hostess's greeting had been nothing but effusive, and he began to wonder if he had made a great mistake in coming at all. The room was already disgustingly full of people—not surprisingly as he had been one of the last to arrive—and he could see at a glance that there was no one here with whom he would usually condescend to pass the time of day. The chances of his even seeing Mlle Deneuve among the crowd seemed to retreat, and he was just wondering when he might without rudeness take his leave when Miss Selina Pinkerton happened to catch his eye.

Sir Robert Lyle was not one of Miss Pinkerton's favourites. Indeed, he had been known on occasion to be quite rude, never to her, but certainly to her brother. The fact that Sir Robert's opinion of this gentleman and her own might happen to coincide did nothing to mitigate the offence, and when she had seen him walk so proudly and disdainfully into the ballroom she had been in two minds about whether to introduce him to Valentine at all. He had a reputation, too, that she could not care for, but he was, after all, so unfairly wealthy! She had just decided he would not do for her Valentine when he apparently became aware of her scrutiny, for he looked directly at her and she was obliged to bow. He was with her in a moment or two, easing his way through the crush in a manner she could only envy, and presenting himself at her side with a bow. She could find no fault with this so she inclined her greying head with a smile, and asked him quite civilly if he had yet had the privilege of meeting her protégée.

He smiled in return. 'The so charming mademoiselle! No, indeed, ma'am, but if what I have heard is to be believed she is charm itself.'

'You are very kind. It is true the child is very sweet; I was quite struck by it myself.'

'I see. You have known Mlle Deneuve long?'

She shook her head, her eyes searching among the dancers. 'Barely three weeks!' She turned to smile at him. 'You think that strange, no doubt! When you meet Valentine I am sure you will understand.'

'I am sure I will,' Sir Robert agreed gravely, thinking that Mlle Deneuve must be even cleverer than he had realised. 'It must be too much to hope that she has a dance left upon her card.'

'I am afraid so,' the good woman concurred proudly, 'but you must meet her nevertheless. Here she is, with Lord Ashby.'

Sir Robert turned. Approaching him was the young exquisite he recognised as the Duke of Carlesby's heir, leading on his arm a young woman. She was wearing a gown of gold crêpe over a slip of white satin. The bodice was cut low and trimmed with lace and seed pearls, as were the tiny puff sleeves. She wore yellow satin slippers and long gloves, and carried a fan of frosted crêpe. Her yellow hair was charmingly braided about her head, and she wore no other ornament than a particularly fine diamond necklace that flashed fierily against the whiteness of her throat.

Sir Robert drew a quick breath. At the Angel Inn she had been a very pretty girl, one that would have turned any man's head. Tonight she was a Helen, one to capture any heart. He nodded to Lord Ashby, and then, as Miss Pinkerton performed the introduction, turned his eyes upon her. She did not recognise him, he was certain. The blue eyes travelled quickly up his person and came to rest upon his face; she smiled, but it was the merest politeness. Galled, he took her extended hand and kissed it, saying with his famous smile. 'Mademoiselle is more beautiful than I had been led to expect. You are to be congratulated, ma'am.'

Genevieve Christy raised her eyes to his face and considered him afresh. For a moment he had confused her. Seeing him at Miss Pinkerton's side she had been at a loss to know why that good lady should be talking to such a country bumpkin; now, when he smiled, she was aware of considerable latent charm; more, of a quite considerable personality, and she was obliged to review her hasty first impressions. Moreover, the name was somehow familiar. She thought for a moment, and then she had it. Lyle. He was old Claudius's great-nephew, the only one of his relations he had wanted her to meet, a man after his own heart he had said, and as rich as a nabob. More money than he knew what to do with, had been the expression. She smiled now, and said to the young gentleman who yet hovered at her elbow, 'My lord, I 'ave such thirst! Could you fetch me a glass of lemonade, *s'il vous plaît*?'

'Of course, mademoiselle, anything at all,' the young man responded with alacrity, casting a look of triumph at Sir Robert. 'It will take me only an instant.'

He was gone in a moment, forcing his way through the crush near the door to the refreshment room, and finally vanished.

Mlle Deneuve smiled. 'Per'aps, m'sieur, you would care to walk a little? I am sure *ma chère* Mlle Pinkerton will not object!'

'No, of course not, my dear, you may do as you wish, naturally.'

Mademoiselle inclined her head, and Sir Robert, who was indeed nothing loath, extended his arm. In a moment they had moved far enough away for Lord Ashby to have little hope of finding them.

'You are cruel to your cavalier, mademoiselle,' Sir Robert said, smiling down at her as they came to a clearer space near the window. 'I trust you do not treat all your partners so.'

She dimpled charmingly. ''E is a boy, m'sieur, no more, and I admit, I find 'is conversation a trifle tedious.'

'He is very well connected, however; you should have a care.'

'*Oui, je sais.* 'E is the son of a duke, is 'e not? 'E told me so 'imself, m'sieur, do you know? 'E thinks it will impress me.'

'And it does not?'

She smiled and shrugged. 'In France there were once many dukes and their sons. They are now mostly dead. But this 'e does not understand.'

'You have but recently come from France yourself, I believe. It must have been very terrible.'

'*Sans doute,*' she agreed, achieving the most artistic shudder. 'But I was, you understand, *le petit bébé*. I can remember but a very little.'

I'll wager you can, thought Sir Robert grimly, but he inclined his head and said, 'Forgive me. No doubt it is not the subject for a ball.' He paused and then said, 'Tell me, mademoiselle, how do you like London? Miss Pinkerton treats you well, I trust.'

'Very well. 'Ow I am fortunate. Everyone is so charming to me, you cannot conceive. And London, ah, it is *charmante* also. Already I am in love with it.'

'Indeed! You have visited the theatre, of course? Kean's *Hamlet* ought not to be missed.'

'Ah, the theatre. No, m'sieur, it 'as not yet been my fortune to attend. 'Owever I always 'ope.'

She smiled up at him, and he responded, saying gallantly, 'I trust Miss Pinkerton will permit me to escort you both one evening. I have a box.'

'That would be delightful, m'sieur. I would like it very much.'

'Good. I shall speak to her of it this evening. Meanwhile, I see your cavalier returning. He does not look vastly pleased. I fear he has been searching the room for you.'

'Ah, the poor Lord Ashby. You are without doubt quite correct. Is it possible 'e will not forgive me?' A dimple peeped mischievously in her cheek as she looked an inquiry.

'Quite impossible, I should imagine, mademoiselle,' Sir Robert responded, kissing her hand. '*A bientôt*,' he murmured. 'Ashby, I return your partner to you. You must forgive us, we have been having the most delightful cose.' He bowed on the words and left them, ignoring the look of wrath cast at him by the youthful Ashby, who yet clutched in his hand the glass of lemonade.

Having considered him to be merely trifling with her Miss Christy was considerably surprised to learn, whilst sitting in Miss Pinkerton's shabby carriage, that Sir Robert Lyle had indeed proposed a visit to the theatre.

'To own the truth, my love,' Miss Pinkerton was saying, 'I was quite in a quandary whether to accept. For in the general way, you understand, he is not a gentleman I should care to be seen with, even if he is from one of our oldest families. You can know nothing of it, naturally, but he has a reputation for, well, not quite nice behaviour, besides being almost *rude* on several occasions I could mention. In fact, I had quite made up my mind to say we were engaged, when it occurred to me that as he had mentioned no particular day I could hardly say such a thing. One does not like to be rude, you know, even to such a man. So I told him we should most likely be delighted, only that he must be prepared for disappointment as our days are mostly full now. And in any case, if you don't quite wish to go I dare say one of us might have a headache, or some such thing, though in the general way I do not like to look quite so particular.'

She paused for breath, and Miss Christy, smiling to herself in the darkness of the carriage, interposed quickly, 'No, no, *chère* Mlle Pinkerton, do not worry on my account. *Je vous assure*, to attend the theatre will be of the most delightful for me. I told Sir Robert this, therefore we must attend, I believe, unless you do not wish it, *particulièrement*?'

'Naturally, child, If you have an eagerness to go we shall of course accept. Though we could always, you know, attend the Play on our own. I have no box, of course, so we would be obliged to ask one of my friends which one does not always like to do—'

'Ah, madame, *je vous en prie*!' exclaimed mademoiselle, laughing, 'we shall accompany Sir Robert Lyle to 'is box. It will be quite delightful, *je vous assure*. Besides, no doubt 'e will assemble a party, and then it will not be so particular. Only consider, madame, we might meet some charming people this way.'

'We might,' Miss Pinkerton conceded doubtfully, by no means convinced. 'But tell me, child, did you not have the most delightful evening?'

They attended the theatre an evening of the following week, Miss Pinkerton having been prevailed upon to accept the invitation for one of their few free days. They had dined first at the Pulteney, having been collected in a most elegant town carriage, but poor Miss Pinkerton was quite dismayed to discover that, instead of making

up a party of ten or more, they were the party themselves
and were expected to attend the theatre with just Sir
Robert Lyle as company. The good lady concealed her
dismay as best she might, but Mlle Deneuve, far from
being put out, seemed to regard the whole thing as a
delightful game. She sparkled her way through the
evening, laughing most of the time, exchanging remarks
with their host as though she had known him all her life.
Miss Pinkerton was a little taken aback, for although
indeed their host was concern itself she would have felt
quite unequal to the familiarity her charge indulged in,
and was forced, albeit reluctantly, to lay it down to her
French upbringing, the first time she had felt obliged to
do any such thing. But then, the child was so clearly
enjoying herself, and if she should managed to capture
the baronet's heart—mentally, Miss Pinkerton reproved
herself. Whatever was she thinking of, letting such
thoughts enter her head? Sir Robert did seem, it was
true, vastly *épris*, but that was just his way; it would be
dreadful if her dear Valentine were to lose her heart. She
forced herself to attend more carefully to their conversation, trying if she could, to be impartial, and soon
discovered, it had to be admitted, that Valentine was
flirting just as outrageously with Sir Robert as he was
with her. For a moment she was shocked, and then she
found herself almost obliged to laugh. The girl was a
minx, there was no doubt about it! She had long since
been aware of the child's intelligence—she was no fool
herself, after all. What was more natural than that she
should play him at his own game? It was probably her
own fault, too, for she had given Valentine a hint of Sir
Robert's shocking reputation and confirmed bachelor-
hood. If he meant her to join that line of despondent
females she apparently had no intention of letting him

get away with it, and Miss Pinkerton could only applaud her. She missed almost the whole of Kean's memorable performance listening to the one that proceeded at her side, but when the curtain fell and she realised with horror that she had attended to barely a tenth of the great actor's speeches, she could not bring herself to feel dismay. All she felt, in fact, was that her protégée was a very cunning little puss, and that Sir Robert deserved all he got.

CHAPTER
FOUR

THE visit to the theatre had, as all three foresaw, inevitable repercussions. The first came on the following afternoon when the Earl of Maland, hearing with dismay that, so far from sending the young Frenchwoman to the rightabout, his sister had actually taken her to the theatre, and sat, which was worse, in Sir Robert Lyle's box, had taken himself hotfoot to her apartment, with the intention, it must be admitted, of reading her a severe lecture. To be sure, Selina had seemed strangely preoccupied when the maid had shown him in, but he had been undaunted, and had launched into his tirade with little more thought. Selina listened, as she should, without interruption, indeed without any remark at all, and it was only when he reached the end of his rehearsed speech that he realised she had not attended to a single word. She was sitting opposite him with her hands folded primly in her lap, and an expression of polite attention on her face, but when he asked what she had to say she made no answer at all, but continued to regard him with that same, he now realised, vacuous expression. The Earl began to grow angry. He had not rehearsed his speech twenty minutes or more to have it pass entirely over her head, and besides, it was really not like Selina to behave in such an impossible way. With a little difficulty he rose from his seat, his corsets creaking, and came to stand over her chair. As he moved her eyes followed him, and she said, in a tone of gentle inquiry, 'Yes, Henry, did you want something?'

The colour suffused the gentleman's face with a rapidity Miss Pinkerton should should have considered alarming. 'Yes, Selina, I did. Tell me, have you heard a single word I have said?'

'Of course, dear.' Miss Pinkerton answered, unperturbed. 'You came to tell me you did not like my attending the theatre with Sir Robert Lyle.'

'Humph. So you heard that, did you?'

'No, I don't believe I did, but I couldn't imagine you should visit me for any other reason.'

For a moment Henry wrestled with himself. His wife, he knew, would tell him he should not permit himself to grow agitated. 'I said that, Selina, and a great deal more. The last time I visited you you led me to believe that that young woman would not be remaining beneath your roof for more than a day or two. Indeed, when I left I was quite hopeful that I had managed to instil some sense into that wooden brain of yours. But what should I discover? Not content with escorting the wench to a ball, wearing our mother's diamonds, you actually accept an invitation from that bounder Lyle and attend the theatre.'

'We had a very pleasant evening,' Miss Pinkerton felt moved to remark.

'Humph! I have not a doubt of it!' the Earl retorted, incensed. 'I dare say the fellow knows how to entertain a lady better than anyone. But that's neither here nor there. What I want to know is, when are you going to get rid of this accursed French female? The whole Town's talking about her, you know, and it ain't what I like.'

'Isn't it, Henry? Well, that's typical, I suppose.'

'What do you mean by that?' her brother demanded, momentarily diverted.

Miss Pinkerton shrugged. 'Merely, Henry, that you have always been nothing but a spoil-sport. If you had but wind that I was enjoying myself you'd stop at nothing to bring it to an end.'

Henry flushed but protested angrily. 'That's dashed unfair, Selina, and quite unlike you. I'm sure I never wish you ill in my life. Only look about you. I'm sure I don't have to remind you that but for me you would not be living in such high style, or indeed living in Town at all. Though perhaps that would have been a blessing, for that—female would doubtless have found someone else to take her under her wing.'

Miss Pinkerton said nothing.

'And as for attending the theatre, in such a particular way, with that fellow Lyle! I may as well tell you, Selina, that if you had that in mind as a match you're fair and far out. Never a more confirmed bachelor than Lyle, I dare say.'

'I had not it in mind, Henry, I can assure you. Valentine wanted to see Kean, and Sir Robert was kind enough to offer us room in his box.'

'Humph! I might believe you, I suppose, had I not heard, on very good authority, that he dined you at the Pulteney beforehand.'

'Eliza Godfry, I suppose,' Miss Pinkerton said without rancour. 'I saw her there. I'm sure she barely tasted her meal for staring at us.'

'Even if it were I see no reason to discredit the tale,' the Earl said in a blustering tone, 'and you do not attempt to deny it, I notice.'

'Whyever should I? As I said before, we had a very pleasant time.'

'But when is the girl leaving, Selina, that's what I want to know?'

His sister smiled at him. 'I really cannot tell you, Henry—not that I would. As far as I'm concerned Valentine may stay here just as long as she wishes. I shall be very glad to have her.'

'It's true. You have run mad.'

'Why? Because I'm enjoying myself at last? You don't understand, Henry, and since I doubt whether you ever will it might be as well if you were to leave.'

'Very well. But you may be sure, Selina, that if you find yourself in trouble over this business you will get no help from me. Indeed not, I wash my hands of the whole affair.'

Having paused impressively for his sister to plead with him he sighed and said stiffly, 'Be so good as to ring for your maid. I shall leave you, Selina, and you should not look to see me back here again until that female has left this house.'

'Very well,' said his sister obligingly, rising to pull the tasselled bell-rope, 'I shall not.'

Some idea of what had passed between them was conveyed to Miss Christy by Miss Pinkerton herself, who announced, on the young woman's entry a few minutes later, that she had always known her brother to be odiously stiff-backed, but that she had never, before that day, actively disliked him.

'I dare say you think that a dreadful thing to say,' Miss Pinkerton added, 'but I shall not repent. I have never liked Henry, I admit it freely, and frankly I fail to see why I should. If I only had funds enough I should pack up this apartment this very day and move into one of my own. Do you know, child, he actually felt obliged to remind me that I was indebted to him for my home?'

Mlle Deneuve was suitably sympathetic, remarking that she had always thought it foolish that one was obliged to care for one's relations simply because that was what they were.

'Exactly! I made sure you would understand. How fortunate it was that I should run into you that day. I do not believe anything so pleasant has happened to me in the whole of my life.'

If she had glanced at her young friend just then Miss Pinkerton might have been at a loss to account for her strangeness of expression, but she did not, and she left the room with her mind perfectly at ease.

Miss Christy herself was forced to endure an interview quite as painful as Miss Pinkerton's about which that lady knew nothing at all. While walking in the park with her maid the young woman found herself hailed, and, glancing up, looked into the handsome face of her brother, high above her on his showy mount. Her abigail, having been in the young woman's company since her earliest years, made a grunt of disapproval, but nodded when Miss Christy said she would see her at the Lancaster Gate, in a half an hour. Master George was a rackety young man, she knew it well, but if he could talk some sense into her mistress he was not without his uses, and she made herself scarce. Watching her go Mr Christy remarked that she looked as sour-faced as ever, and, swinging himself from the saddle, proceeded to lead his horse at her side.

'You must have a care, George,' his sister told him severely. 'If anyone should hear you address me so—'

He grinned. 'They won't, don't you fear. And by the by, it ain't George any more.'

'It isn't?'

He shook his head. 'The Honourable Frederick

Winthrop, ma'am, at your service. You might try not to forget it,' he added with rather a sly glance.

'I won't, but is the Honourable not rather a risk?'

'Devil a bit!' her brother answered airily. 'Gives one a bit of tone.'

'Maybe, but what if someone should try to check up on you? Who are you supposed to be?'

'Well, to be frank with you, sis, I haven't quite decided. But that's neither here nor there, as you well know. What I want to know is, what the deuce do you think you're playing at? Surely you know Lyle is old Claudius's nephew? What if he should rumble you?'

'He won't, and of course I knew.'

'You say "he won't" easily enough, but I really don't believe you've thought it out, and that ain't like you. Chances are the old gager told his family all about you. Have you thought of that?'

'Of course I have,' his sister answered rather crossly, 'but how can he possibly connect Mlle Deneuve, lately arrived from Paris, with the piece his elderly uncle had been courting in Bedfordshire? It's hardly likely, George, you must admit it. Besides,' she added, 'I've not yet decided if he's my target.'

'Have you not, indeed! If you want to make me believe that, you'll have to stop attending the Play with the fellow, at the very least. Indeed, I can't think what you were about getting the tattle-mongers talking about you in such a way.'

His sister blushed, but said, 'As it happened, George, I particularly wanted to see Kean, and Miss Pinkerton has no box. Besides, he gave us a very pleasant evening.'

Her brother shot her a searching glance. 'I say, Gen, this ain't like you at all. I hope to goodness you're not falling for the fellow.'

Miss Christy was moved to laugh. 'Falling for him? No indeed. He's supposed to be confirmed bachelor, George, that's all. Think what a conquest it would be, a man like Lyle, who has resisted all the caps that have been thrown at him, succumbing to a rig like mine!'

'Famous,' agreed Mr Christy somewhat dryly. 'I just wish you might have a care, that's all.'

'Oh fudge,' said his sister, growing cross.

His excursion to the theatre came very soon to the ears of Sir Robert's cronies at White's Club, and he was subjected on his next visit to those hallowed precincts to some severe ribbing. He bore it all in good part, however, and since no one could believe Sir Robert to be serious in his intentions the matter was very soon allowed to drop. Lady Lyle might have been moved to make several rather waspish comments about her stepson's behaviour, but no one dared to repeat them, and even if they had, it is doubtful whether the gentleman would have cared. When it was discovered, however, that the gentleman had called in Brunswick Square some two days later to invite the young woman for a drive, that lady felt sufficiently moved to send for her son, and ask him what the devil he thought Robert was about.

'Robert?' repeated the young man with a frown. 'I neither know nor care. No doubt she is merely his latest flirt. I wonder you let it worry you.'

His mother, a wilting creature who still possessed a certain elfin charm, raised herself from her position of artistic collapse.

'Worry *me*!' she exclaimed, justifiably incensed. 'I should have thought, Joseph, that you would have been mightily concerned yourself. What if he means to cut you out?'

The young man laughed, and moved to where he

could examine the perfection of his cravat in a little gilt mirror. 'Cut me out? Robert? Devil a bit! I dare say the thought has never entered the fellow's head. The man's a confirmed bachelor; there ain't a woman alive who could persuade him to the altar, you can take my word for it. As far as I can see, the succession is as safe as ever, and if he keeps burning the candle as he has been doing I shan't have to wait so very long, either. Or perhaps even one of his accursed horses might settle it for me before that.'

'Joseph!' In spite of her feelings on the subject Lady Lyle was moved to protest. 'That is hardly seemly, Joseph. I must beg of you to remember yourself. Robert is your brother, whatever his faults, and I'm sure I for one hope he lives to a very great age.'

'Rot,' said her son simply, turning away from his reflection to look at her. 'You know as well as I how pleased you would be if the news came of Robert's death. I call it dashed hypocritical of you not to own it.'

'How can you talk to me in that odious way! I am your mother, you would do well to remember! I admit Robert and I have not always seen eye to eye, sometimes it is inevitable. No doubt he resented me heartily, especially since when I married your father I was only a very little older than Robert himself. But for me to wish his death—it is unthinkable.' To do her justice, Lady Lyle had been hugely shocked.

Her son, however, merely smiled. 'You say that now, mother, but how would you feel if he were to die? How would it be if, tomorrow, you could live just as you were used, if we could go to Dearing in the knowledge that it was mine and not his, and that there would be sufficient wealth for both of us to live as we have always wished? Would you not like it excessively? Of course you would, and you're a fool if you don't own it. However,' he continued, carefully dusting his blue sleeve, 'I don't mean to argue with you, over this or anything. You may take it from me that Robert has no thought of marriage in his head, and if you can only manage to outlive him we might be able to enjoy his fortune at our leisure.' Moving to her he ran one finger across her cheek. 'You worry too much. You're getting wrinkles! I don't like that, mother, you should have a care. And that mirror of yours, you should get rid of it. It ain't flattering at all, makes one too thin in the face.'

Bending, he kissed her fleetingly, and then, with a curious curl to his rather full mouth, took himself away. Lady Lyle lay back upon her lilac sofa and pressed her hands to her temples.

Sir Robert Lyle appeared to be enjoying himself, meanwhile. He and Mlle Deneuve were seen by everyone to be getting along famously, and one or two even began to speak of Sir Robert's imminent downfall. Already he had eclipsed the hopeful Lord Ashby as the most prominent of mademoiselle's court, and even the sceptical were able to detect that in the baronet's expression that they had never before observed.

'Depend upon it,' Mr Pendleton said to his friend Lamley, 'it's a case. Charles has bet a pony upon it with Dacres.'

'Then he's a fool,' Lord Lamley opined calmly, taking snuff with a practised air. 'Lyle ain't the marrying kind. For some reason or other it amuses him to play the love-sick calf, but it ain't real, believe me. In my opinion it's all aimed at that stepmother of his. She don't like it above half, that's plain to see.'

'Hmm.' Mr Pendleton considered this new idea. 'Then it's all a ruse, you think, just to upset Lady Lyle?'

Lord Lamley nodded. 'And her son. To be honest

with you, Pendleton, I can't but admit that they deserve it, for a more avaricious pair I don't believe I ever met. I dare say Joseph Lyle never looks at his brother without adding up what he's worth.'

Lord Lamley's opinion was shared by several, but those guessing at a marriage predominated, so much so that Miss Christy was moved to remark, when she stood up for the second time with Sir Robert at Almack's one evening, that if they were not careful people would start to talk.

The gentleman smiled down at her. 'Shall you care for such things, mademoiselle? I had not thought it would matter to you.'

'*Mais non, c'est fort amusante*. Very amusing. Only we know there is nothing in the stories.'

'Nothing at all, mademoiselle? You distress me. I had thought we were becoming good friends.'

'Ah, so we are, m'sieur, indeed. This I did not mean. Your friendship I value greatly, but very well I know that you are not the kind of gentleman who will marry. It would be very foolish of me, would it not, m'sieur, to mistake your intentions?'

She smiled up at him as she spoke, her blue eyes enormous and appealing, containing an expression Sir Robert had not seen before. He hesitated a moment, and then said slowly, 'Perhaps they are not so very wrong, mademoiselle.'

She frowned, apparently at a loss to understand him. 'M'sieur?'

'Nothing. Forgive me. Look, do you see that exquisite young gentleman who is eyeing us most particularly?'

Miss Christy turned her head. 'By the door? 'E wears a very fine waistcoat!'

'Doesn't he,' Sir Robert agreed dryly. 'That, my dear

mademoiselle, is my brother. You must permit me to introduce you.'

The young lady wrinkled her brow. '*Votre frère*? Forgive me, but is 'e not very young?'

'The son of my father's second marriage. He, more than anyone, would wish me to remain unwed.'

'*Vraiment?*' She looked at him with brows raised. 'Me, I think I shall not like to meet this gentleman.'

'Oh, he is perfectly polite, I assure you. Quite a paragon, in fact. But I betray myself. Come, I am sure he longs to be introduced to the so charming Mlle Deneuve.'

The young lady would have protested, but he took her firmly by the arm and led her from the set, and in a moment she found herself being extravagantly bowed to by the perfect young gentleman.

Since she possessed a brother who fancied himself to be in the height of fashion Miss Christy was not totally unused to the crazes and foibles of the young, but she found in Mr Joseph Lyle's manner something almost objectionable. It was not his bow, though it was so low she might have been royalty, or even the smile he then bestowed upon her. Nor could she find the aforementioned waistcoat, startling though it certainly was, something to take exception to. Rather it was his eyes, the cold way in which he examined her from head to toe, making her feel he was adding up the total cost of her apparel, and the obsequious way in which he then said he was utterly delighted to make her acquaintance. To be sure, he was all that was polite, and smiled at her and Sir Robert a very great deal, but life had taught her young and she knew well already how to assess a character in a moment, and she could not care for his. Of all the people she had met in London she would trust this one the least, and since she was inclined to like Sir Robert for himself as well as his money she found herself wishing he were not so closely connected with this particular little toad. She said all that was proper, however, expressing her delight to be in London, saying she would be charmed to see Mr Lyle any time he should wish to call to take her for a drive.

'I only wish, m'sieur,' she said as they walked away, 'that 'e may not 'ave meant what 'e said.'

Sir Robert smiled. 'What was that, mademoiselle?'

'That 'e would call one day to take me for a drive in the park.'

'Should you not care to go? He is a capital whip, I assure you, quite unlikely to overturn you.'

She eyed him frankly, wondering briefly just how far she could go. 'To be honest with you, m'sieur, I would always fear 'im, I think. 'E 'as the eyes of the fox, so cruel and cunning. Me, I could not trust 'im.'

'You do not offend me,' he answered shortly.

'*Oui*. Forgive me if I offend, but I must speak 'ow I find.'

'You do not offend me,' He answered shortly. 'Come—' here he smiled at her again—'shall we rejoin the set or would you care for some refreshment?'

'Some lemonade, yes. I think I am tired of the dancing just now.'

Accordingly they left the floor, and in a moment or two Sir Robert, having carved a way through the press on the floor, had disappeared into the refreshment-room.

From his position near the door Joseph Lyle observed their departure with a frown upon his handsome brow. When his mother had broached the subject of his brother's marriage he had dismissed the suggestion out of hand. It was clearly ridiculous, his mother was just being over-dramatic as usual. Now, however, he felt it would be necessary to have a care. There was that in his brother's eyes he had never before observed, a certain tenderness, a softening of the hardness he usually affected, that Joseph could not like and that unaccountably disturbed him. He began, extremely reluctantly, to wonder if his mother had been in the right after all. What if Robert, after all these years, should decide to marry, if only to cut him out of the succession? If the situations had been reversed he would not have hesitated to take such a step; indeed, he would probably have done it years before, and been the father of several sturdy sons already, but he had never suspected such a thing of Robert, for, it had to be admitted, it was not his style. What if, however, he should discover in the French piece something he had found nowhere else, and should, indeed, be tempted to change his state? The idea was one he could not tolerate. Too long had he lived upon the expectation of inheritance, and had even, of late, been idly considering ways of hastening his accession. To see it all vanish would be highly unpleasant, and he had no intention of letting such a thing occur. Something would need to be done, he saw it clearly, and preferably before things got out of hand. There were two things he could do. He had no doubt of his charm; already a succession of broken hearts lay behind him. Chances were the lady would quickly succumb to the charms of a much younger, more fashionable man than his brother, and if there should be a little rivalry, well, what woman did not thrive on that? But besides this there was Mlle Deneuve herself. His idle inquiries had elicited the information that nobody knew any more about her than that she had but lately come from France. It had been enough for society that she was a guest of the Honourable Miss Selina Pinkerton. For Joseph Lyle, however, this was by no means sufficient. Suspicious by nature, it occurred to him now that there could be much in Mlle Deneuve's past that she would not care to have revealed. If he could only discover what she could perhaps be persuaded to leave his brother alone, and turn her attentions to some person less closely connected with Mr Joseph Lyle.

CHAPTER
FIVE

Since his arrival in London the fortunes of Mr George Christy had fluctuated. He had soon found himself lodgings in a select part of St James, and had set about establishing for himself a past. A desire to impress had led him to attach an Honourable to his name, but even before his sister had suggested it he had been wondering if this had been foolhardy. Already one or two of his acquaintances had been making idle inquiries about his background, and although it had been no more than a passing curiosity, easily fobbed off, it had aroused his alarm and shown him the necessity of being more cautious in future. In the past he had left all such things to his sister, and she had made it seem so easy, there had never been the slightest awkwardness over their identities, that he had had no doubt of his ability to do the same. Now he was acquiring a new respect for his sister's capabilities, and was beginning to wonder if he had been too hasty in his decision to start on his own. Determination, however, came to his rescue. His sister had chosen for herself a very fat proposition indeed; he had every intention of doing quite as well for himself, if not better, if only he could decide how.

There had seemed plenty of time at the beginning. He had chosen for himself a name, and a vague background, but that was all, and with this had sallied forth to enjoy himself upon the Town. He had provided himself almost at once with a new set of clothes, choosing from Mr Schultz several coats of extremely fashionable cut and cloth, that would make quite a hole in the money he had got from old Claudius. Then there were the new waistcoats it was essential for him to possess, the glossy new hessians, the indispensable curly brimmed beaver to crown his new haircut. A selection of fobs and seals was *de rigueur*, and until he had provided himself with a Malacca cane he could not feel himself to be properly attired. The fact that no one had asked him for the money at the time had made him quite drunk with the beauty of it all, and if he suffered an occasional anxious moment about the day when the bills started to arrive he was well able to banish the thought and turn his attention to the tables.

George Christy had always fancied himself as something of a master at the game of piquet, and so far those chance acquaintances he had made had done nothing to make him change his mind. To be sure, he had lost rather heavily one evening after a day at Newmarket, but that had been pure bad luck and had not since been repeated. A pleasant young man with considerable careless charm he had rapidly made himself a number of friends, and was very soon introduced to many more. He found himself invited to card parties with some regularity, and since he soon showed himself a keen gambler also went with friends to such places as the Whitehall Cockpit, where he rubbed shoulders with ostlers and sweeps, and to Newmarket, where he was privileged to squander his blunt on some of the year's best horseflesh. Since his friends showed no alarm at all in the betting of several hundred guineas on a single race he was persuaded to follow suit, but his choices always seemed to be ill-fated, tending to stumble and break their legs, or run so slowly that they were fortunate if they did not come last. His friends suffered similar reverses which they greeted in the most careless and cheerful manner, and Mr Christy was persuaded to regard his own heavy losses in a similarly unconcerned way.

Of all his numerous acquaintance there was one with whom he felt a particular affinity. Lord Francis Dinmore, eldest son of the Duke of Cranleigh, had soon detected in the Honourable Frederick Winthrop a kindred spirit. Like himself Mr Winthrop seemed to have money to burn and an inclination to do it wildly with little thought for the consequences. Lord Francis was the son of an indulgent father, blessed with an allowance that staggered most of his friends, and the knowledge that whatever scrape he should find himself in his father, although indeed disapproving, would shortly be on hand to redeem him. He thought little of punting five hundred guineas on a single horse, laughing when it cantered home at the end of the field, exclaiming cheerfully that he had never had an eye for horseflesh and that he would probably recover the whole at hazard that evening. His unconcern was infectious, as were his perpetual good humour and ready smile. The two found themselves quickly drawn, and within a day or two of having met seemed in a fair way to becoming intimates. Lord Francis was a member of Watier's, as well as a number of other select establishments of a similar nature, and soon discovered that the Honourable Frederick would greatly appreciate the opportunity of entering one of these clubs. Lord Francis might be a wild young man but his credit was excellent, and he was, moreover, the son of one of the country's more wealthy, and eccentric, noblemen. Consequently when he appeared at Lady Wantage's one evening with a youthful-looking gentleman of whom no one knew anything at all, not an eyebrow was raised, nor a question asked. The fact that none of the more regular visitors to the house had ever set eyes upon this particular young buck did not seem to matter, and the Honourable Frederick was permitted to take his place at the table with the rest.

Lady Wantage held select gambling parties most evenings of the week in a modish establishments in Half-Moon Street. It was her policy to send out cards of invitation to a favoured few, but no one who was introduced was ever turned away, particularly if it seemed as though he might have a few hundred guineas to lose at faro, or hazard. It was here, about three days after his first appearance there, that Sir Robert again encountered the young man from the Angel Inn. He recognised him instantly, for indeed it had for some time been a mystery to him what had happened to the gentleman. Confident that he would not be recognised he took his seat opposite him at faro and spent the rest of the evening watching him lose money. He was drinking rather freely of Lady Wantage's excellent brandy, betting recklessly as the night wore on. The flush mounted in his cheeks and the sparkle in his eye grew, but his hand remained steady, as did his voice. At his side Lord Francis was a steady loser and a cheerful one. Soon his notes of hand began to pile up at Lady Wantage's side, but he was quite unconcerned, Sir Robert noticed, unlike his young friend. Mr Christy too was punting on tick and pushed across the table quite as many notes of hand as Lord Francis, but his smile was not so cheerful, nor his lip, when he asked for the sum of his losses, so steady. Sir Robert himself had been a moderate winner; in fact he rose from the table with an additional two hundred pounds, but this was a rare event, the Bank winning nearly every time. He sat on after Mr Christy and Lord Francis had taken their leave and began to wonder how long it would be before Miss Christy found her young relative importuning her for funds.

In fact he had already done so. Genevieve, meeting her young brother by appointment one afternoon in the park, had been disturbed by his casual request for fifty guineas, not such a large amount, and she had had it to spare. What had concerned her more was the fact that George had apparently already run through what they had had from Claudius Lyle, but her questions on this subject were greeted with irritation and an assurance that his financial embarrassments were trivial and temporary. Genevieve had tried to think no more about it, but the subject remained with her and when, some five days later, he had asked her for a further fifty guineas she had known quite serious alarm.

'I'm sure if I had thought you would quibble about a paltry fifty guineas I should never have asked you,' Mr Christy complained as they strolled together down one of the public walks. 'It is not such a very great thing, after all, and this rig I am running requires that I have ready funds available.'

'What is it you are doing, George?' Miss Christy tentatively inquired. 'Do you know you have never told me?'

'Well, it is quite secret, Gen. You know yourself how it is. What if I should tell you and then you let it slip? Not that you would, of course, but there's no saying what might happen if you only grow careless.'

'I should hope, George, that I am past growing careless,' Genevieve remarked, slightly hurt by his offhand tone. 'However, I do not mean to pry, and if you are sure everything is quite under control, well, I'm sure I do not grudge you the money.'

'I knew you would not,' George exclaimed, looking at her warmly. 'Do you have it about you now? I don't mean to push you, only it would be extremely convenient if I could have it for this evening.'

'Of course I don't have it about me now. If you really need it urgently, however, Mary may bring it round to you. I believe I have that amount in my room.'

'Thank you, Gen,' George said with what his sister considered was inordinate relief. 'Not that it would have signified greatly, you understand, but it will be a great deal more convenient this way.'

'Of course, George.'

'And you need not fear that I shan't return it, for I shall, and more besides, I make no doubt, once everything is running smoothly.'

'Of course, George,' his sister repeated, smiling up at him as naturally as she felt able.

Mr Christy's fortunes continued to waver. The second fifty guineas went, not to pay some of the young gentleman's mounting debts, but, like the first, across the table at one of London's more select gaming establishments. For a few days Mr Christy's luck seemed to have changed. While his sister's first loan had vanished without trace in a very short space of time the second proved more fortunate, and for a week or more Mr Christy found himself to be relatively plump in the pocket. The thought that he would have done well to pay off some of his creditors occurred only to be dismissed; since his luck had plainly changed he would do far better, he knew, to place the whole sum on an outsider at Newmarket, about which he had had certain information that it could not lose.

Genevieve did not see her brother for more than a fortnight. Her time had been so taken up with the growing round of social engagements that she barely had leisure to do more than think occasionally about her brother and to trust that fortune was at last smiling upon this wayward young man. She was beginning to regret her sanctioning of his exploits. He had yet to tell her exactly what he was about in Town, and the suspicion that he had no definite plan could not but occur. She began to reproach herself for thinking him capable of taking care of himself, but he was of age, and she could not be protecting him forever. When she did see him he presented himself in Brunswick Square at an hour when he knew Miss Pinkerton to have stepped out. He was ushered into her presence as she sat in the elegant drawing-room and startled her into uttering a stifled gasp. She controlled her amazement, however, until the door had shut upon the maid, but then, jumping up, hurried forward to demand what he meant by presenting himself in so particular a manner.

'Had no choice, Gen,' he told her bluntly, running one hand through already disordered locks. 'Had to see you, and could not be forever riding in the park. Dash it all, you might never have walked there.'

Miss Christy had had leisure by this time to observe her brother's altered looks and harassed expression. He had apparently had very little sleep of late for dark shadows ringed his handsome eyes and furrows she had never noticed before were etched between his brows. 'George!' she exclaimed, guiding him, unprotesting, to a chair. 'Whatever has occurred? Are you ill?'

He laughed shortly. 'No, Gen, rolled up.'

'Rolled up?' his sister repeated blankly.

'The devil's been in the cards, Gen, and that dashed

horse—But that's neither here nor there. The thing is, I need five hundred guineas without delay.'

'Five hundred?' repeated his sister, sitting down on the nearest chair. 'You mean you are in debt?'

'Haven't I just told you so?' he answered, irritably eyeing her. 'Lord, Gen, I never knew you to be so slow. The thing is, when can you let me have it?'

'Five hundred guineas?' Miss Christy said again, unconsciously pleating her handkerchief in her lap. 'Dearest, I do not have it.'

'Not about you, of course, I see that. But when can you let me have it?'

'George, dearest, I do not have that much left.'

He stared at her. 'How is that?' he demanded, considerably annoyed. 'I don't know what you can have spent it on, and I know for certain that you have given me only one hundred.'

'I know, but there have been expenses, gowns, and so on. I have some left, it is true, but not more than two hundred, of that I am sure.'

'That ain't enough,' her brother told her frankly. 'The thing is, if I'm not to end up in the Fleet I must have that five hundred and without delay. Even with that I dare say I shall have to leave any number of bills unpaid, for I owe my tailor nearly three.'

'Then what is the money for, George? Whatever have you been about?'

'Lord, I don't know!' exclaimed her brother, rising and taking several hasty steps about the room. 'I'm sure if I had thought you would prose on at me in that dashed way I should never have come.'

'If you wish me to pay you five hundred guineas I think I have a right to know what for,' his sister told him reasonably.

'Why, when I have no doubt but that you wouldn't understand in any case?' He sighed, and then said wearily, 'The thing is, I owe a bit of money to a fellow who held the Bank at Lady Wantage's last evening. And then there is my debt at Tattersalls, though that ain't due for a week or more yet, and the chances are by that time I shall have effected a recovery. But this fellow Chalgrove, well, I may as well tell you, Gen, I don't like to keep him waiting above a day or two. Debt of honour, you know. Not the thing.'

Her brain reeling, Genevieve tried vainly to take in what her young brother so calmly revealed. 'Then in fact your debts amount to a great deal more than five hundred,' she said faintly.

He glanced impatiently at her. 'I dare say, but I've told you, I shall make a recovery long before they are due. Only give me the five hundred and the thing will be right.'

'George, I don't have it.'

'Well!' exclaimed her brother considerably put out. 'If that don't beat all. If you ain't been making up to that fellow Lyle for the past month I don't know what you have been doing. What the devil are you waiting for? It never took you a month yet to trap 'em. Don't try to tell me you're losing your touch, for I shan't believe you.'

'No, it isn't that. It's just—in short, George, Sir Robert isn't like the others. I have to be careful he doesn't tumble to what I'm about.'

'You mean he ain't hooked? From what I heard he more or less lives in your pocket these days! Why, they're even taking bets on it, you know.'

'Bets?' Miss Christy exclaimed, revolted. 'How odious men are.'

'Well, I never heard you say so before, but that's

neither here nor there. The thing is, Gen, you could help me if you wanted to, I know that well enough. It seems to me you've grown dashed particular of late if you don't want to help your brother out of a spot of trouble. Dash it all, do you want me to give 'em all the bag? I dare say I could do it, for I'm not without practice, as you know, but it ain't what I like, and besides, I'd rather taken a fancy to living in London.'

'No, no, you must not do that,' his sister exclaimed, wringing her hands distractedly. 'I shall find some way, only you must give me a few days.'

'Well, I suppose I could,' her brother conceded magnanimously. 'You said you had two hundred guineas left. Give me that, and I dare say the thing might not be so very bad.'

'George, it's all I have.'

'Well,' he exclaimed disgustedly, 'if that don't beat all. I'm sure if I had thought you would kick up a dust over a paltry two hundred I should never have come. A fine thing it is if a man can't ask his sister for help, that's all I can say.'

'Well, I suppose you must have it, though I hope you will discharge some of your debts, at least.'

'What do you take me for?' her brother demanded crossly. 'Haven't I told you that's what it's for? Anyone would think you wanted me to have a run.'

'Of course I don't, and indeed I had thought perhaps—' She stopped, and then said, 'But I must admit that you worry me a little when you talk so easily of money and debts of honour. I only hope you know what you're about!'

'Well, you may be easy on that head,' he told her grandly, 'for I dare say I shall finish with a great deal more than you, and without all the bother you've had as well. And you needn't think I shall forget you, for I shall not. In fact,' he added magnanimously, 'If you need any help in your present caper I shall be only too glad to oblige.'

'Thank you, George,' his sister said, smiling warmly at him. 'Wait just a moment and I shall fetch you what I have.'

She rose as she spoke and quitted the room. Her brother, having listened for a moment to her footsteps in the passage outside, walked quickly to where her reticule lay on the armchair. Opening it he emptied it without conscience onto the table, and rapidly possessed himself the coins therein. Then, having refastened it and set it back upon the chair, he was about to take up his position again by the fireplace when a small silver snuffbox, cunningly inlaid with mother of pearl, lying on the mantelshelf, caught his eye. In a moment he had snatched it up and slipped it into his pocket. When his sister returned with the money he was lounging at his ease in one of Miss Pinkerton's faded chintz armchairs. He rose quickly as she entered and pocketed the roll of bills she handed him, and in a very few minutes had taken his leave, saying he had no desire to explain his presence to Miss Pinkerton on her return.

CHAPTER
SIX

IT was three days before Miss Christy saw Sir Robert again. She had spent those days in a fever of anxiety about her brother, hoping he might, once again, cast caution to the winds and visit her in Brunswick Square. She was destined to learn nothing, however, passing her days in abstraction and listlessness that caused her hostess to look askance at her more than once. When finally Sir Robert called in Brunswick Square he found Miss Christy seated alone in the drawing-room, some embroidery on her knee, at which she attempted to give an impression of having been working. The start she gave when he entered unannounced, springing up and allowing the unfortunate embroidery to fall to the floor, rather led him to believe her attention had been desultory. For a moment he had thought she was about to throw herself into his arms, and was surprised; then she had apparently recollected herself and begged him to be seated.

Sir Robert had absented himself as part of a deliberate policy. His observations of Mr Christy had led him to believe it would not be long before that young buck was applying to his sister for aid, and he wanted Miss Christy to have had plenty of time to consider her position before he again put in an appearance. That she had been greatly worried was at once apparent. She seemed to have lost weight, and dark circles Sir Robert had not seen before now ringed her lovely eyes. Briefly he was tempted to take her into his arms and tell her not to worry about anything. It was the recollection of her duplicity that made him hesitate and seat himself in one of Miss Pinkerton's chairs as though he had noticed nothing amiss.

For a while the young lady attempted polite conversation. She smiled at him as much as ever, laughed at his jokes, parried his thrusts, but Sir Robert was not deceived. She was a great deal concerned, and the gentleman rather thought that, had he not been there, she would have been pacing the room in her anxiety. Having listened politely for some minutes to her lively description of a ball he had not attended he interrupted her without compunction, saying as he rose from his chair, 'Mlle Deneuve, I wish you would tell me what is troubling you.'

She gave a start. It was true, she had found her rôle increasingly difficult to maintain that afternoon, but had so prided herself on her ability to carry off any deception she had not thought Sir Robert could have seen through her so easily. Reminding herself once again that it would not do to underestimate this particular fish she sighed, and smiled up at him as he stood over her.

'It is true, m'sieur, I am a little worried, but it is of no great matter. Please do not concern yourself.'

He contemplated her with a seriousness she did not know. 'Mademoiselle, if you are worried about something how may I not be concerned? Three days ago when I saw you you were in perfect health. Now, after so short a time, I find you looking quite hagged—I do not mince words, you see—and you expect me not to be worried?

Come, mademoiselle, I had thought you counted me your friend.'

'And so I do,' she replied, rising and walking quickly about the room. 'Only I do not see how you may be of any assistance.'

She had forgotten her accent, but Sir Robert gave no sign of having noticed. Instead he crossed swiftly to where she stood, agitatedly wringing her hands, and took them within a warm, comforting grasp. 'Do you trust me so little? Pray tell me what it is. There is no saying what I might not be able to do if only you would confide in me.'

For a moment she hesitated. There was that in Sir Robert's face she had seen once before, and almost it emboldened her to speak. Her natural instincts told her she was too premature; it was the recollection of George's difficulties that made her swallow her misgivings.

'Sir Robert, what can I say? You will think it so odious of me.'

'I assure you I shall not. Tell me what it is.'

She sighed and withdrew her hands gently from his grasp. 'Money,' she said, baldly.

For a moment he did not answer. She had turned away from him as she spoke and had her back to him, but he had thought momentarily that she had an extreme reluctance in making this statement. Forcing his mind ruthlessly back to his Uncle Claudius he hardened his heart once more and said gently, 'Indeed?'

Without looking at him she nodded. 'It is so stupid. *Vraiment*, I do not know 'ow this thing 'as 'appened. One moment there is, ah, plenty, and then—' She shrugged her shoulders expressively. 'M'sieur, what can I say? There are only debts, debts, and more debts.'

'I see.' Thoughtfully Sir Robert moved to stand before the fire, and Miss Christy eyed him covertly from beneath her lashes. 'Miss Pinkerton, may she not help you?'

'M'sieur!' Miss Christy had given a laugh of genuine amusement. ''Ow may I ask madame such a thing? 'As she not 'oused me, fed me, knowing nothing of me? *Vraiment*, I believe she has very little money 'erself, enough for 'er needs, no more.' She sighed and turned away. 'No, m'sieur, I may not ask Mlle Pinkerton, and I should not 'ave mentioned the matter to you. Forgive me. I wish you would think of it no more.'

'You expect too much of me, mademoiselle.'

Glancing up, Genevieve saw that he had turned and was looking at her once more with that strange expression in his eyes. 'M'sieur?'

'You have told me this tale of woe, and you expect me to forget it? I am not so paltry a fellow, believe me!'

'Indeed, m'sieur, that is very kind of you, but what may you do? *Naturellement*, I appreciate your concern, but I do not see 'ow you may 'elp me.'

'You may give me your bills.'

For a moment she seemed truly surprised. 'My bills, m'sieur? 'Ow may I do so? Surely you do not think I would let you settle them? *Vraiment*, it is indeed most kind of you, and you must not think I do not appreciate it, but—'

'But what, mademoiselle?'

'M'sieur, I cannot do such a thing! For me to take money from a gentleman, almost a stranger, *non, ce n'est pas possible*!'

'Of course it would be,' Sir Robert said, taking snuff in a leisurely manner, 'were I not to make you offer of my hand.'

'Your 'and?' she repeated, almost as though she had not understood him.

'Why not? For me to pay my wife's debts must surely be quite unexceptional.'

For a moment she stared at him, and then she laughed. 'M'sieur, you cannot be serious. You 'ave no intention of marrying me.'

'How do you know? Can it be that you have not noticed how I feel about you?'

'M'sieur, I do not know. Pray do not, I cannot think.' She pressed her hands to her cheeks, and Sir Robert noticed with interest that they trembled. It reminded him of what a very good actress she was, a timely recollection.

He said calmly, 'I have been too sudden. I admit, when I called here today I had no idea that I should make you such an offer, but if you believe me to be merely trifling with you, let me assure you, mademoiselle, that I was never more serious in my life.'

She shook her head. 'M'sieur, I do not know what to say, I 'ad thought—you seemed—in short, m'sieur, I thought you enjoyed my company greatly. We laughed much, *c'est vrai*, we 'ad much fun, but that you might 'ave serious intentions towards me I did not consider.'

'Then I pray you, mademoiselle, consider it now, for I would have you believe, however hard it might be, that I desire nothing more in this world than to make you my wife.'

'But m'sieur, this is very strange. *Vraiment*, if I 'ad not told you of my—small problem you would not 'ave made me this offer. 'Ow, then, may I believe that you really wish to marry me, that you are not just trying to oblige me?'

She was seated on the very edge of the chair, her blue

eyes enormous in her strained face. For a moment Sir
Robert contemplated her as she stared up at him, and
then, in one swift movement, had knelt at her side and
caught her hands in his. 'It is true, when I came here
today I had no intention of making you such an offer.
Indeed, I did not know exactly how things stood with
me. But you may believe, mademoiselle, that I desire
nothing more than to make you my wife, and can
only thank you for making me aware of my own feelings.'

'M'sieur, I do not know what to say.'

'It is quite simple, child. Yes.'

She shook her head. *Je ne peux pas.*

Sir Robert sighed and released her hands. 'I see. Your
feelings are, in fact, not engaged. Very well. Forgive me.
I should not so have importuned you had I realised.'
Standing up, he shook out his coat-tails and smiled down
at her. 'It was very foolish of me, was it not? Come, let us
forget about it, it is of no great matter.'

'No, m'sieur, do not go, *je vous en prie.*'

Sir Robert had bowed and made to leave the room,
but now he turned and, with a strangely sinking feeling
in his breast, said, 'Mademoiselle?'

'Do not go. I will—if you truly want me I will marry
you, m'sieur.'

If she seemed strangely disconsolate Sir Robert did
not notice, gaining her in two rapid strides and kissing
her hand. 'You mean it?'

She nodded, and forced a smile to her lips. *'Oui,*
m'sieur,' she whispered. 'I will marry you.'

He did not try to kiss her, for which she was profound-
ly grateful, but he pressed her hands in a most speaking
way and let her know she had made him the happiest
man in the world.

'Thank you,' she said in a small voice. 'I will do my best to be a conformable wife.'

An impartial observer might have laughed at this point, Sir Robert, fortunately, was far from impartial, and appeared not to notice the particularly forlorn note in this utterance, or, indeed, Mlle Deneuve's suddenly improved command of his language. He merely kissed her hand again and released it, saying in a businesslike tone, 'Tell me, is there anyone to whom I must apply for your hand?'

She shook her head. 'No, m'sieur, there is no one.'

'In that case I shall send a notice to the *Gazette* without delay. You will, of course, wish to be married at once.'

Her eyes swung to his. She repeated in a faltering tone, 'At once?'

'Of course. Your debts, mademoiselle. Surely you had not forgotten?'

'Oh. My debts. No, m'sieur, I 'ad not forgot. You wish that I should marry you first?'

He smiled down at her. 'Do you find that so very odd? It would be a great deal more proper, mademoiselle, and I own I have a great dislike of parting with my money to someone who is not a relative. No doubt my brother would tell you I have the greatest dislike of it in any case, which may be true, I know not. In this case, certainly, I think it would be better if we were married first. I should not care to have you abscond as soon as your debts are settled.'

He spoke lightly, but her eyes flew to his face, and he realised he had been too blunt. He smiled, therefore, and said, 'Forgive me, I know you will not do so. I am simply so anxious not to lose you, my love, that I will do anything to keep you.'

'You will?'

He nodded. 'Do you blame me?'

'No, m'sieur, I suppose not.'

'Good. You will leave the arrangements to me, then? You will naturally wish for some of your friends to be present—'

'No!'

'I beg your pardon?'

'No, m'sieur, there is no one,' Genevieve said, recollecting herself.

'I see. Not even Miss Pinkerton?'

'Mlle Pinkerton? I know not. Per'aps. Must I tell you now?'

'Of course not, sweet, but do not delay too long. You have no idea how much I desire to call you my own.'

Joseph Lyle had not been idle. His seemingly casual inquiries had revealed that Mlle Deneuve had proceeded to Brunswick Square from the Pulteney Hotel, where the greasing of several appropriate fists elicited the information that she had arrived, quite unheralded, one evening in February, and that she had been accompanied by a young gentleman riding escort. At this Mr Lyle raised his brows. The information was interesting, but as yet he could not see how it might be turned to account, except that it was apparent that Mlle Deneuve was not as friendless as she would prefer everyone to believe. Whence she had come, however, no one at the Pulteney could tell him. Nor had anyone, it transpired, heard of the young lady at the French Embassy. A family Deneuve had been known, it was true, but it was generally believed that the whole tribe had perished on the scaffold, in the grim years of the Terror. If this Mlle Deneuve were one of these she must have been a veritable babe at the time, and somehow escaped. Mr Lyle considered this for some little time. It was possible, he had to admit it, but somehow he found it hard to believe. As astute in his own way as Miss Christy herself he had soon discovered something not quite true about the young lady, although as yet he had been unable to decide what it was. He resolved, therefore, on the afternoon of his brother's gallant proposal of marriage, that he should take the young lady for the promised drive.

Contrary to what one might expect Miss Christy was not to be found in elated spirits on the afternoon in question. As soon as Sir Robert had left her to her own devices she had closeted herself in her chamber, there to indulge in a hearty bout of weeping upon her bed. She had arisen red-eyed but calm, and once more in control of her emotions. The whole morning had been a vastly unpleasant experience. That she had missed Sir Robert in the three days of his absence she had not admitted even to herself, and to discover, as he knelt on one knee before her, that there was no one in the world she would rather marry had really been quite disturbing. A very little reflection had served to show her how impossible the whole situation was. She had deceived him totally, of this she was sure. If he had had the slightest idea of what she had really been about there would have been no hope for her at all. For her to admit her deception was quite out of the question. For a wild moment she had considered telling him everything, but the thought of George and his difficulties had rapidly brought her to her senses. It was quite impossible. She had chosen Sir Robert as her target, and it was really most foolish, after all this time, to allow herself to be led astray by a maidenly fancy. Somehow, and within the shortest possible space of time, Sir Robert must be persuaded to part with five hundred pounds at the very least, and if she could only do this by marrying him then marry she must. That she would be obliged, then, to flee was an unpleasant necessity. Once he knew the truth Sir Robert would want nothing more to do with her. Better by far that she should disappear from his life forever.

That her reasoning was confused and clouded by her emotions did not occur to her, and the news that a gentleman had called brought her from her chamber with hope in her breast. The thought that it might be George made her run down the passage in anticipation; to enter the room and find Joseph Lyle nearly made her burst into tears. Long practice came to her aid. Smiling pleasantly she stepped forward with her hand outheld, expressing her very great pleasure at seeing the young gentleman again.

Mr Lyle was not deceived. That she was expecting someone quite other was perfectly obvious to him, as was the fact that she had been greatly disappointed. As he delivered his invitation, therefore, there was an ice in his heart he had not previously known, making him more than ever determined to thwart the ambitious little fortune-hunter in front of him. She had hesitated visibly before saying she would be delighted, and he suspected there had been something of a hunted animal in those beautiful eyes. But she had left the room to fetch her wrap with apparent eagerness, and Mr Lyle felt in his veins the thrill of the hunt, the keenness of the foxhound that knows it is on the trail.

It was a fine afternoon, but crisp, and it was with a shiver that Miss Christy allowed herself to be handed into Mr Lyle's splendid curricle. There was something about the gentleman she could not like, something that made her wish to be anywhere but in his company, and when he solicitously spread the blanket across her knees she had felt an almost physical revulsion. Telling herself she was being quite nonsensical she schooled her features into an expression of polite interest, and tried to stop herself from wondering how long she would be obliged to tolerate his company. At first it seemed as though it might not be so bad after all. The afternoon was so very fine, the sky so clear, it was a pleasure to be outside even in such company, and when she observed how well Mr Lyle handled his high-spirited horses she began to wonder if she could have misjudged him. The curricle was so well sprung, too, it was a delight to travel in, quite unlike those sporting carriages she had travelled in before generally driven by some young blood more anxious to impress, and caring little as a result for his passenger's comfort. There was only one other gentleman of her acquaintance who handled the ribbons quite so well, and she had resolved not to think about him.

Joseph Lyle had been at some pains to put the young lady at her ease. That she mistrusted him he could not doubt, but he found that he did not greatly care. He meant to discover what she was about, and by any means that might be open to him.

'Tell me, mademoiselle,' he said, as he swung out to pass a dawdling landau, 'how long have you been in this country?'

'Two months, m'sieur,' came the cautious reply.

'I trust you find our hospitality to your liking.'

'Most certainly. Everyone has been most kind.'

'You have been most fortunate in your patroness, it has to be admitted. But you knew her before, I believe, prior to your arrival in England?'

He was not looking at her, being intent at that moment in guiding the carriage between a stationary tilbury and a barouche coming quickly in the other direction, but Miss Christy was instantly on her guard, saying easily, 'No, m'sieur, I did not meet Mlle Pinkerton until after I was resident in this country.'

'Then you came here knowing no one at all? How very brave of you.'

'Not really, m'sieur. I 'ad been invited to live with an old friend of my mama. Unfortunately when I arrived I found she 'ad died but the week before.'

'How very distressing.'

'I did not know 'er, you understand, but it was a little awkward, for I 'ad intended making my 'ome with 'er, now that my parents are dead.'

'I see. You were fortunate indeed to have found so kind a lady as Miss Pinkerton. Without her one imagines you would have been quite homeless.'

'Yes, m'sieur, quite.'

'How very distressing,' Mr Lyle repeated, turning his head to look at her for a moment. 'But tell me, mademoiselle, what do you propose to do now? You may not, one supposes, make your home forever in Brunswick Square.'

'No, m'sieur, that I 'ad never intended to do.'

'In fact,' Mr Lyle continued as though giving the matter his careful consideration, 'there would seem to be only one course open to a young lady of breeding, assuming you do not wish to tread the boards or become some whelp's governess.'

She looked an inquiry. 'M'sieur?'

'Marriage, mademoiselle! Pray do not pretend to me that you have not considered such a thing.'

'No, m'sieur, I pretend nothing.'

'I am so glad. I particularly wished for us to understand each other from the very first. It makes everything so much easier, don't you think?'

'*Certainement*, m'sieur,' Genevieve said, apparently quite unperturbed.

'Good. I made sure you were an amenable female. How nice it is to be proved right.'

'*Pardon*, m'sieur, I believe I do not perfectly understand you.'

'You may drop the pretence, young lady, I think. You are no more French than I, and I do wish you might give me credit for just a little intelligence.'

Certain now that she should never have come on this drive Miss Christy said in a tone of mystified inquiry, 'M'sieur? I think I do not understand what you say.'

'Cut line, if you please,' Lyle said, his good humour evaporating fast. 'You need have no fear of my telling anyone, for I shall not. I dare say, if you had not cast your lures at my brother, I should have been very pleased to let you be, for I ain't above appreciating a cunning caper myself. But you see, my dear, I have expectations myself from that quarter, and I don't mean to see a harpy like you cutting me out. I dare say you don't realise how things stand, but I'm Robert's heir, and I mean to remain so, whatever it might involve. So I tell you to your head, miss, it won't do. Forget about my brother, and you'll do well enough. There are plenty of other willing fish about, you've no need to take this particular one. But I don't have a choice. He's all I have. So, leave him alone, and I dare say we'll both survive.'

'I see. And if I do not?'

Lyle smiled. All trace of an accent had gone, but Miss Christy had spoken without a tremor, seemingly quite unperturbed. 'If you do not, mademoiselle, I shall have no hesitation in telling everyone about your little deceit, particularly Miss Pinkerton, and we shall see then who might be persuaded to marry you.'

'I see. You would leave me little choice, in fact.'

'None whatever, Miss—whatever your name is. I am so pleased to find you so utterly in agreement with me.'

Genevieve was silent. Indeed, she had nothing whatever to say, merely wishing herself back in Brunswick Square, that she might have opportunity to think.

CHAPTER
SEVEN

ON leaving Brunswick Square Mr George Christy had proceeded directly to a small shop in the city, one whose dirty windows made it almost impossible to see inside, but with which the young gentleman had previously had quite satisfactory dealings. When he had caught up the silver snuff-box from the mantelshelf it had been no more than the action of a moment; having had time to consider he decided it would be better for all concerned if he disposed of the little piece as quickly as he possibly could. There could be no doubt of its value: the workmanship was such as was rarely seen in those times; had he not been so very hard-pressed he might have been sorely tempted to keep it for his own use. Now, however, only one course seemed to be open to him. Standing, as he did, in urgent need of funds he could only sell it, and this he intended to do without delay.

The door to the dingy shop opened with its customary squeak; George was always surprised when no cobwebs were to be found festooning it on the inside. As usual the interior was stocked with a great variety of items, some pawned by temporarily impoverished young gentlemen of fashion, the majority acquired in a much more questionable manner by the proprietor in the early hours of the morning, brought to him by worthies who would certainly not have been seen near the shop in the cold light of day. Within the shop could be found almost anything one had set one's heart on, but George never came there to buy.

As usual he was conscious of very careful scrutiny, although as usual, he could see no one. He suspected the owner, an extremely cautious gentleman of semitic origins, of possessing some spyhole through which he considered his customers, but while this necessarily discomposed the young gentleman he refused to be perturbed, waiting patiently until the owner should consider his scrutiny complete. After a minute or two this worthy seemed satisfied for a door at the back of the shop opened and a hunched individual, wearing a rusty black coat with tails long enough to sweep the floor, shuffled his way into the light. Despite his study of George through the peep-hole he seemed to retain considerable misgivings about his character for he approached with exceeding slowness, dragging his slippered feet on the dusty floor and regarding George out of a pair of extremely shrewd grey eyes. As usual George found himself considerably at a disadvantage although he could never decide why, and raised one hand to the ordered neckcloth that seemed of a sudden to have grown too tight. Eventually the old man spoke, his voice scarcely more than a whisper, yet strangely disturbing in the almost oppressive silence of the little shop.

'You have something for me?'

George nodded, and produced the box from his pocket. Taking it in a mittened paw the old man took from a capacious pocket a small eyeglass and unhurriedly contemplated what he had been given. To George this invesitigation seemed to take an uncommonly long time, but the old man appeared satisfied at last, for he dropped the box and glass together into his pocket and said with a smile, 'Fifty guineas, young sir.'

'Fifty!' ejaculated Mr Christy, fingering his neckcloth again and turning rather red. 'It's worth a great deal more than that. I had thought a hundred at the very least.'

The old man laughed, leering up at George from beneath jutting brows. 'Do you think me as big a fool as yourself? If that box was honestly come by you may call me King George. Stolen, that's what it was, as were the other things you've been so obliging as to bring me. Well, I'm not such a fool, young sir, let me tell you. Chances are there's quite a few swells who would care to know what has happened to their little treasures, and I've a mind I know where some of them came from, too. A hundred guineas! You'll take the fifty and be satisfied with it, or you're an even bigger fool than I took you for. A hundred guineas!'

Very flushed, George spluttered that the box was honestly come by, and if the old man would only give it back to him he'd take it to someone who could appreciate its true value.

'Yes, and finish in Newgate, I make no doubt! You should not be so greedy, my friend. There are many who would not give you even half of that. Be grateful for what you can get.'

George bit his lip. He was sorely tempted to tell the old fellow to keep his miserable fifty guineas and return to him his box, but he knew of no one else who would give him money without question, and was besides much inclined to think that the highly unpleasant gentleman he had narrowly avoided earlier in the day would be awaiting him on his return to his lodgings. Raising his chin a little, therefore, and summoning as much pride as he was able, he signified his willingness to accept the old villain's offer, and waited impatiently while this worthy shuffled back into his hidden stronghold.

On leaving the shop George felt a little better. Fifty guineas was better than nothing, after all, and if only he could once more avoid the fellow from his tailor he might contrive to pass a very tolerable evening. He was engaged to attend a card-party with some friends, and before his visit to his sister had thought he would have to cry off, for not only had he been totally without ready funds, he was also in debt to nearly all of them for various sums. Now, however, all was different. He had never doubted his ability to save himself in the end, and began to envisage a time in the very near future when he would be able to tell his sister to keep her money, besides returning the two hundred guineas that reposed so snugly in his pocket. Never one to dwell over-long upon his misfortunes he was whistling as he strolled down the street, mulling pleasurably over the various ways of tipping the tailor's cove the double.

His mood, when finally he left for his party, was one of considerable elation. On returning to his lodging he had found his man, Collins, awaiting him at the corner of the street with the intelligence that the tailor's johnny was seated in the vestibule and showed no signs of being persuaded to leave, at least not without a considerable sum as compensation reposing in his pocket. The faithful Collins had, therefore, so far prevailed upon one of the kitchen maids that his master was able to enter his establishment by means of the back door, which he did without delay, to the delighted giggles of the maid, with whom Collins seemed very familiar and called Becky. Consequently the tailor's johnny was left to kick his heels in the vestibule for the rest of the day, uneasily aware that he had been duped, but unable to decide quite how.

George's party that evening was to take place in the house of one of his numerous acquaintances, a gentleman known as Offery who owned a large house in Berkeley Square. A gentleman of about fifty, he was a confirmed bachelor with a gambler's soul, and such parties were far from infrequent, generally lasting well into the following day with considerable sums of money exchanging hands. To be invited to one was considered by many to be a mixed blessing, for his lordship was known to possess a quite uncanny skill with a deck, generally robbing a great many more of his guests than might have been thought proper. By dint of plying them with the best burgundy at his supper, and the finest brandy afterwards, however, he managed to fill his table without difficulty, and if some of his contemporaries had grown wise enough to avoid these evenings, well, there would be many wild young men only too willing to take their place for his lordship to feel over-concerned.

George had never been fortunate enough to attend before, and when the little gilt-edged invitation had arrived at his lodging one morning he had felt himself finally to be well-established, unable to realise that it were merely his apparent carelessness with his blunt that had persuaded my lord to invite him at all. He had dressed with more than usual care, sending his man to press his coat a second time as there had been the merest suspicion of a wrinkle in its sleeve, and taking almost an hour over the tying of his intricate cravat. He had sauntered into the street very well satisfied, however, and confident that with the two hundred and fifty guineas just then in his possession he would be able to enjoy a tolerable evening's entertainment.

Such pleasurable anticipation was slightly marred on his entry to his lordship's sombre dwelling, for he arrived barely half a minute before another guest, and had only just been relieved of his hat and gloves when my Lord Chalgrove was admitted. Although he might reasonably have expected to encounter this gentleman that evening he had been able to push such an unpleasant occurrence to the back of his mind. It seemed the action of a very cruel fate to remind him so soon of his obligations towards this particular gentleman. Lord Chalgrove, however, seemed to be in jovial mood. His eye might sparkle a little when it lighted upon the Honourable Frederick Winthrop, but he greeted him with a smile and asked him lightly whether he had hopes of repairing some of his recent losses.

He was about to answer non-comittally when it occurred to George that his lordship might just have offered him a most pleasurable way of being relieved of one of his more pressing debts. A disastrous evening's play at Lady Wantage's the day before had seen Lord Chalgrove relieve him of more than three hundred of his precious guineas. He had given his note of hand with a careless smile and a request for a day or two's grace, but although Lord Chalgrove had accepted the note without question there had been that in his eye George could not quite like, and he had decided that to fall foul of this gentleman would perhaps be very foolish indeed. Now, however, an excellent plan occurred to him, one which, if successful, as he had no doubt it would be, would not only settle this debt of honour but possibly all the others as well, not to mention satisfying the johnny still waiting, he supposed, at his lodgings. Consequently he smiled. Lord Chalgrove was an inveterate gambler, how could he refuse?

'My lord,' George said, waiting while the gentleman was relieved of hat and gloves, 'I wish you would give me the opportunity of a little revenge.'

'Indeed?' responded his lordship, contemplating the young gentleman shrewdly from beneath deceptively lazy lids. 'In what particular way?'

'You are a gamester, my lord, are you not, like myself? Surely you would not refuse me!'

'What had you in mind, Winthrop?' his lordship inquired, carefully flicking an invisible speck of dust from his immaculate sleeve.

With an access of friendliness George took his arm and they proceeded up the stairs in apparent good humour and companionship. 'You play piquet, my lord, I believe? Last evening you held the Bank, the odds were heavily in your favour. Will you deny me the opportunity of a little revenge? I must tell you that I regard piquet as very much my own game.'

'Do you indeed,' Chalgrove responded with an apparent growth of interest. 'Almost you tempt me.'

'Almost?' George laughed easily. 'Surely, my lord, you are not craven? I had believed you possessed a gamester's heart, do not tell me I have been misinformed?'

Chalgrove smiled slightly. 'No, Winthrop, you were not. It is just—in short, my friend—I do hope you will not be offended—I had hoped for something with a little more—ah—spice this evening.'

'Perhaps I may oblige you there, too, my lord,' George responded, forcing himself to ignore the delicate snub. 'I am prepared to offer you odds.'

'Indeed!' my lord replied, glancing again at the handsome face beside him. 'Of what kind?'

George smiled. 'Shall we say two to one? Will that add sufficient spice?'

For a moment the gentleman seemed to ponder within himself. Beside him Mr Christy wrestled with his growing impatience. It would never do for this insufferable fellow to see how greatly he had put him out. Finally, as the drawing-room was reached, Lord Chalgrove drew away his arm and turned to face the younger man. 'Very well. You have persuaded me. Shall we say after supper?'

George bowed. 'I shall look forward to it, my lord, you may be sure.'

'Undoubtedly,' his lordship responded, dismissing the young man with a casual nod that made George long for a sword at his side.

At first the evening began well. A number of gentlemen sat down to play at faro, but George was called upon to make up a fourth at whist, which he did with some relief, having no desire to lose all his money before he could play Chalgrove. At supper he was a modest winner, and so encouraged by the apparent change in his luck that he went into the dining-room with his spirits high. The fine burgundy and the excellence of the supper rather contributed to his elation, and consequently, when he took his place opposite Chalgrove in the early hours of the following morning, he felt as though nothing could prevent him from recovering everything. He had heard much about Chalgrove's skill at cards, but did not doubt that he would be his master. His lordship began cautiously, too, taking some time over the consideration of his discard, thus permitting George to believe he had the beating of him. The first rubber went his way, and by a quite substantial margin, so that when the lackey approached with an offer of brandy he pushed his glass forward with a smile, confident that nothing now could prevent his winning.

For a further rubber or two the play continued in his favour; glancing at the tally George saw that he was quite substantially ahead. To be sure, Lord Chalgrove did not seem particularly disturbed by this fact, but then he was a hardened gamester, and had besides so large a fortune a mere three hundred guineas could mean nothing at all. He began to grow careless in his discard; the fourth rubber went Chalgrove's way, but by so small a margin George hardly heeded it.

Thereafter, however, George's luck began to change. So convinced was he that he was Chalgrove's superior he failed to compute the odds as he ought, so that when, after another rubber or two, he chanced to glance at the tally again it was with a shock that he discovered his lordship to have drawn very slightly ahead. His own lead had seemed so unassailable for a moment he thought the tally must be incorrect. Swift reckoning revealed no mistake. Frowning slightly he pushed the brandy glass from him, and refused the lackey when he next approached. Attempting to affect a recovery he was more cautious than before, taking time over his discard, trying to anticipate his opponent's move, but always, now, Chalgrove seemed to possess the balance of the cards, and George realised he had been duped by a very clever player indeed. Cursing himself for a fool he tried desperately to recover the lost points, but gradually Chalgrove drew from him, until he realised that here he had a player immeasurably better than himself. It was a discovery that galled, and also humiliated him. The fellow was so insufferable, how dare he trick the Honourable Frederick Winthrop in such a way? If he were not very careful George would be forced to show him he had yet some tricks remaining.

Thus the idea took root. At first George dismissed it as impossible. Lord Chalgrove was no tap-room acquaintance, but a member of society, with a position of some standing. If he were discovered it would be the end of everything. The lackey passed with the brandy again, and this time George permitted him to refill his glass, catching it by the slim stem and draining it at once. All would depend on the next rubber. If he won all would be well. If he lost—

Once again they cut for deal. With a sigh of relief he turned up a higher card and relaxed a little, certain that fortune was with him once more. In a voice that trembled slightly he declared a point of five, certain Chalgrove could not beat this. Almost in disbelief he heard the declaration of a point of six, and by the end of the rubber realised he no longer had any choice. He had declared odds against himself, he must needs do something.

Thereafter the game went entirely his way. Mr Christy's hand might tremble slightly as he picked up his cards, but Lord Chalgrove soon discovered that he no longer had any intention of losing. Once he frowned sharply, and directed a look of wonderment at his opponent. He said nothing, however, not even when the final rubber went against him and he realised the Honourable Frederick had soundly beaten him. Rising, he straightened his wrist-bands and contemplated the young man from between idle lids.

'My congratulations, Winthrop. You have the beating of me, it must be admitted. Sometime you must let me know how it was done.' The voice was polite, and a lazy smile curled his lordship's thin lips, but there was steel in the grey eyes and a look of almost implacable hatred that quite startled Mr Christy. For a moment he wondered if Lord Chalgrove really suspected him, but then he dismissed it. Was he not a master, taught by one of the best? He smiled easily as he stood up.

'I held the cards, I think. I must thank you, however, my lord, for offering the chance of revenge.'

'The pleasure, sir, is entirely mine.' With a rapid glance he totalled the sum of his losses, and then said pleasantly, 'Three hundred you owed me, I think? The balance, then is a little over four hundred guineas.' From his pocket he pulled a fat roll of bills and proceeded to count them rapidly onto the table. When he had finished he glanced up with his lazy smile and said pleasantly, 'You are the winner tonight, Winthrop, but have a care. I do not permit myself to be so beaten more than once.'

George was pocketing the bills with some speed, but he looked up sharply at this, alerted by his lordship's tone. But the expression was as idle as ever, the grey eyes almost hidden beneath the heavily drooping lids. His lordship bowed then, ironically George thought, and moved away to join a group by the fire.

Thereafter the evening went well for George. With his debt settled and money in his pocket George felt able to play without restriction, and this he did, even managing to win quite handsomely at the faro table. About him other men were winning or cheerfully losing; the brandy went round the table unchecked, most of the gentlemen possessed of rather flushed cheeks. One of these, a buck as young as George himself, appeared to have drunk rather more than was good for him, for he was talking loudly and making a number of ribald comments to his cronies. Generally they laughed, but there was an occasional awkward silence which the young gentleman appeared not to notice, scribbling his vowels and

pushing them across the table with the greatest unconcern imaginable. George knew him slightly, but he was
not a particular friend, having, as George himself said, a
great deal more hair than wit. With a curl of disdain on
his lips he watched as the young gentleman lurched
across the table, and it was at this moment that a pin, an
elaborate affair with several diamonds set around a very
large sapphire, became dislodged from his cravat and, as
he flung back against the chair, dropped to the ground.
George opened his mouth to comment, but then he
hesitated. Glancing about him it seemed as though no
one else had noticed, certainly not the young man
himself, who was just then draining his brandy glass, and
spilling quite a considerable amount onto his satin knee-
breeches. George bided his time. The company was
gradually becoming more and more noisy; already one
gentleman had fallen asleep across the table and had had
to be aroused before the game could continue.

At last the young man seemed to have had enough.
Swaying a little he pushed himself up from his chair, and
announced that it was time he sent for his carriage. As
two of the friends rose hurriedly to support him George
bent down, and, under the pretext of fiddling with his
shoe, caught up the pin that lay upon the carpet and
concealed it in his palm. Straightening up he glanced
about him and then, satisfied that no one had observed
him, contrived to slip it into his pocket. It was at this
moment that he became aware of a particularly close
scrutiny from across the room and turned to stare full
into the no longer lazy face of Lord Chalgrove.

For a moment George could not breathe. Lord Chalgrove had not moved, nor spoken, but he was regarding
him with such an expression of accusation that George
could not doubt that he had seen. The room seemed

uncomfortably hot, and he raised one hand to loosen his neckcloth. Afterwards he was to curse himself for a fool. Whether it was the brandy or simply his own confidence in himself that betrayed him he could never be sure, but instead of rising instantly and returning the pin to its owner he watched transfixed as Lord Chalgrove approached him and demanded in a voice of ice that he turn out his pockets.

There was a sudden hush. Chalgrove's voice, raised as it was, had fallen with deadly impact upon the whole company, so that they turned as one to stare, first at Chalgrove himself, and then at George. Mr Christy had gone very red, and did not move as Chalgrove approached him and repeated his request. Then, as his wits returned, he demanded what the devil his lordship meant by such an insulting remark.

'I believe you know, Winthrop, well enough.'

'No, I say, Chalgrove, it ain't good enough,' protested his horrified host, rising quickly and coming to George's side. 'Not done, my good fellow, not done at all.'

'Keep out of this Offery,' Chalgrove answered quietly. 'Melbry, I'd be grateful if, before you leave us, you were to check on your sapphire pin.'

The young buck, who, with his escorts, had been standing horror-struck while this went forward, started, and peered foggily into the folds of his cravat. 'Gone,' he announced, in tones of wonder. 'Must have dropped it.' Swaying slightly he made to search about him on the floor, and had it not been for the supporting arms of his friends he would soon have ended on his face.

'Yes, Melbry, you dropped it, but you won't find it there. In fact, had I not happened to be looking in a certain direction I dare say you would never have seen it again.'

'I say, Chalgrove,' Lord Offery exclaimed, rolling his eyes at his friend, 'I do think you ought to explain yourself. Seems to me you're a trifle foxed.'

His expression grim Lord Chalgrove turned once more to Mr Christy. 'What have you to say, Winthrop? Will you turn out your pockets, or must I do it for you?'

'Steady, Chalgrove,' said a calming voice in his ear.

'Well, Winthrop?' his lordship persisted, not taking his eyes from George's flushed countenance. 'Have you nothing to say?'

George raised his chin a little. 'I protest I do not understand you, my lord,' he said as calmly as he could.

'It is quite simple, my friend,' Chalgrove said, throwing off the restraining arm and approaching him in rapid strides. 'Like you I saw Melbry drop his pin. I was sure you had noticed it too and could not think why you said nothing about it. I would have spoken, but something told me it would be much better if I did not. Several of my friends have been missing small items lately, snuff-boxes and the like. It occurred to me that if I held my peace I might discover what had happened to these trinkets, and I believe, Winthrop, that I have.' He was beside him now, and before George, or indeed anyone else, realised what he was about, he had plunged his hand into George's pocket and produced, together with a large bundle of notes which he tossed to one side, Melbry's sapphire pin. In the hush that followed the sound of the jewel falling onto the table was unexpectedly loud, and the company looked as one to George for an explanation. After instinctively stretching out his hand to retrieve his notes he hesitated, and withdrew the hand. He was quite silent.

'I dare say I should have suspected you from the first,' Chalgrove continued quietly, his voice heavy in the silence. 'There are no Winthrops that I know of in Northumberland, so I wrote to a friend of mine, asking if he knew of you. The Honourable Charles Winthrop told me that, as far as he knew, there was no Honourable Frederick. So just who are you, my friend, besides a card-sharp? Who are you, eh?'

Still George made no answer. At Chalgrove's side Lord Offery who was slowly collecting his wits, said quietly, 'We'll have the Watch, I think, William. This is no matter for any of us.'

Slowly his lordship drew himself up. 'You're right,' he said shortly. 'We have witnesses to what happened. Fetch the Watch by all means.'

George Christy held himself very straight. There was something nightmarish about the whole situation, and, as in a nightmare, he could not quite believe he would not wake up and find it all a dream. Nothing like this had ever happened to him before; in all his imaginings he had coped with the most dreadful situations in the calmest manner; now, all his intuition deserted him. He was dimly aware of someone dispatching a lackey, and also that one or two of the other guests had managed, in the coolest manner, to position themselves by the door. The rest of the company seemed disposed to treat the matter as casually as possible, encouraged by their host, who shepherded a number of them back to their tables and saw them re-established at their games. George himself remained standing, as did Lord Chalgrove, watching him as though he knew he would disappear at the slightest opportunity. Gradually, however, George's senses began to return. They were on the first floor, this much he remembered, and there was a wide window just before him, heavily curtained. Never having been in Lord Offery's residence before he had no idea what was beyond this, but his senses told him that it was the back of the house, with the chance of a balcony and garden. His fear receding slightly as he considered his chances of escaping, he glanced coolly at Lord Chalgrove and said with his easy smile, 'You will not object, my lord, if I sit down? I must confess to being slightly wearied by this business.'

Lord Chalgrove said nothing. Having waited a moment for his reply George shrugged, and then moved in an offhand manner to where a chair stood with its back to the window in question. Then, in the most casual manner he could assume he draped himself in it and searched in his pocket for his snuff-box.

From where he now sat he had a clear view of the room and its occupants. Thanks to Lord Offery the majority of guests were now occupied once more with their gaming, and even the two gentlemen who lounged in the doorway seemed to have a great deal more interest in the faro table than in the Honourable Frederick Winthrop. Only Lord Chalgrove remained obstinately watching him. As George stretched himself in the chair he drew up one for himself, but even as he sat down his eyes did not leave George's face. For some minutes, for as long, in fact, as he was able to curb his impatience, George sat unmoving although he expected every second to hear the fall of heavy boots upon the stairs as the lackey returned with the Watch. Lord Chalgrove also did not move, except once, when a cry of success from the faro table instinctively made him turn his head. In a trice George was out of his chair and through the gap in the curtains. As his fingers encountered the coldness of glass he heard the cry behind him, and then he had discovered the latch and turned it. Chill night air caressed his cheeks, his boots echoed hollowly on the wooden boarding of a balcony, and he reached out both hands to the railing he could but dimly see. Behind him someone wrenched the curtain aside. As the light flooded the balcony he turned his head briefly, trapping for a second only a vista of angry, shouting faces; then, in a single movement, he had vaulted the rail and dropped to the garden below.

He landed with a sickening crack. The drop had been far greater than he had supposed, and although his feet sank deeply into the softness of recently turned soil the sound of breaking bone was unmistakable, followed as it was by a flooding pain that threatened for a moment to deprive him of his senses. In a second he was up, however, spurred by shouts above him and the sound of running feet. Even through his pain he knew he held an advantage; no one who knew the extent of the drop would have attempted it, but, with a limb surely broken, could he turn such an advantage to his own use?

With a strength he had not known he possessed George began to drag himself across the garden. Dimly, now, he could determine a high stone wall before him—somewhere, please God, there had to be a gate. Behind him the shouts of outrage had ceased; vaguely he supposed they were all making their way with some haste to the ground floor, it would not be a minute before they were upon him. Frantically glancing about him George could see no way of escape. Fear and desperation had almost blotted the pain of his broken leg from his mind; he had always thought of himself as protected from that which threatened the common man; to find himself now so exposed would be chastening indeed, had he the leisure to consider it. Even as it was, the thought that this could not be happening to him persisted, as did the belief that something must occur to rescue him from it. It was at this moment that the gate, previously hidden from him by a stout bush, became visible near the back wall, and he dragged himself towards it with increased speed. The handle was old and rusted, but it yielded at a touch, and he found himself on some kind of cobbled yard. There was a smell of horses and the occasional muffled snort, and he realised he had found his way into the mews. With an effort he pushed shut the rotting gate; then, as sounds of pursuit echoed behind him in the garden, he turned, and with as much strength as his weakened state would allow hobbled away into the darkness.

CHAPTER
EIGHT

THE general outrage following George's disappearance was quite sufficient to reach the ears of Sir Robert Lyle, even preoccupied, as he was, with arrangements for his forthcoming marriage. Indeed, Chalgrove proved so vociferous in his indignation that it seemed the whole Town must know of it, and Sir Robert wondered how he would find Miss Christy when he saw her next. Since his proposal, the last time he had seen her, he had provided himself with a special licence, but his general air was one of deep gloom, not usually associated with one about to enter voluntarily upon the married state. In fact, he had made sure he had given very little thought to the matter. The possibility that he might have let himself become more entranced than he had intended by Miss Christy's manifold charms could not but occur to him, and it was a sobering reflection that, at the advanced age of thirty-seven, he could succumb like a schoolboy to the attraction of a beautiful smile. No longer did the catalogue of Miss Christy's many faults serve to banish this feeling; he had long since forgotten the anger and indignation he had known in Bedfordshire when he had promised his uncle that he would bring her back. The only way, now, to oblivion was a period of riotous living, and he was generally to be found in the early hours of the morning whiling away the time at one of London's more raffish

spots, a glass of brandy at his elbow and some pretty
dancer in his arms. This ploy was not always successful,
however, for when he slept it was Miss Christy who filled
his dreams, and not the pretty painted creature with
whom he had spent the last few hours. When the news of
George's defection reached him he had raised his brows,
and, knowing it could not be long before Miss Christy
sought him out he presented himself one evening at
Lady Grantham's soirée, secure in the knowledge that as
this female was one of Selina Pinkerton's bosom-bows
Miss Christy would almost certainly be in attendance.

She was, and he saw at a glance that she was not in
health. The fine bloom that had characterised her had
fled, to be replaced by a haunted expression in those fine
blue eyes that worked uncomfortably on Sir Robert's
self-control. He noticed from across the room that her
eyes were rarely still, that she seemed continuously to be
looking for someone, and he wondered, suddenly if she
had managed not to hear what was being said about her
brother. Since he could not imagine her to be looking so
earnestly for anyone else this seemed to be the case, and
indeed, when finally he approached her and bowed she
seemed so very much startled by his presence that he
could not flatter himself that he had been the cause of
her distress. Distractedly she greeted him and made
room upon the sofa. Indeed, she looked so very distressed that all thought of duplicity fled as Sir Robert
took her hand and said earnestly, 'Mademoiselle, whatever has occurred? Are you ill?'

For a moment he thought she had not heard him, for
her eyes still darted about the room. Then, growing
aware that her hand reposed in his she drew it quickly
away saying with a smile, '*Pardonez moi*. I did not 'ear
what you were saying.'

'Nothing of any importance, believe me. I asked merely whether you were ill. It is perhaps a little too hot for you?'

'It is 'ot,' she conceded, 'but I must confess to being a little concerned. You must forgive me if I make a poor conversation.'

'If it is the same thing that troubled you before I have to tell you, mademoiselle, that I am in possession of a special licence. Only give me the word. We may be married as soon as you choose.'

'A special licence?' Disconcerted, she turned quickly to him. For a moment he thought she was about to tell him something, and hope sprang in his breast, but then she seemed to recollect herself and shook her head. '*Vraiment*, m'sieur, I cannot think of it now. You are right, I am a little unwell. Do you see Mlle Pinkerton anywhere? I think I should like to go 'ome.'

He was on his feet at once. 'I will be as quick as I can. I believe I saw Miss Pinkerton just a moment ago, talking to Lady Jersey.' He was gone, and Miss Christy was left to contemplate whatever preoccupied her until Miss Pinkerton joined her in a very few minutes with her wrap over one arm.

'Dear child!' she exclaimed, peering with some anxiety into Genevieve's face, 'Sir Robert tells me you are ill. I thought myself that you were looking a trifle pulled when we left but you seemed so anxious to attend. However, let us take our leave. I dare say it is no more than the headache, after all.'

Distractedly agreeing that her head did pain her Genevieve rose, and in a very few minutes they had taken their leave and were seated in Miss Pinkerton's shabby town carriage.

'I do trust it is nothing serious, Valentine,' Miss

Pinkerton said, with an anxious glance in Genevieve's direction. 'There has been a great deal of influenza about lately, and I should not wish to think you had succumbed whilst in my care.'

'No, madame, I am sure it is no more than the 'eadache. *Sans doute*, I shall be better tomorrow.'

'I hope so, indeed,' Miss Pinkerton returned, although her tone clearly betrayed her doubt. Too long for her liking had her dearest Valentine been without her bloom.

They completed the journey in silence. Too preoccupied with her own affairs to make conversation Genevieve barely noticed where they were, and it was with a start that she heard Miss Pinkerton speak to her again, with the news that they had reached Brunswick Square. A night of restless tossing followed. A little calm reflection after her conversation with Joseph Lyle had shown her the folly of her recent actions. There was no need for her to marry Sir Robert Lyle, and much though it irritated her to have to bow to Mr Lyle's demands, a flight from the metropolis would solve both George's problems and her own. She had resolved to tell George so when next she saw him, though with a heavy heart, and be gone from London before Sir Robert could seek her out again. This happy plan had been forestalled. No word had come from George. A messenger sent to his rooms had returned with the disturbing news that the Honourable Frederick had not been seen for three days, and her maid, Mary, told her that Mr Collins was greatly concerned. She had gone to the soirée that evening in the vain hope that her brother might attend. She returned to Brunswick Square with no notion of what she should do next. Sleep, disturbed by dreams, came with the dawn. She awoke to the sound of her curtains being drawn, and opened her eyes onto a morning as grey as her own feelings, and as depressed. For a moment or two she watched as her maid bustled about the room, laying out her gown and petticoats, and then with a great effort she sat up in bed and pulled her wrap about her shoulders.

'So you're awake, then, miss,' Mary said, coming to stand by the bed. 'There's a message come this morning, brought by a nasty dirty boy, who said a girl gave 'im a shilling to bring it here.'

Genevieve looked up sharply. 'A message? Give it to me!'

In her haste she almost snatched the crumpled and grubbied piece of paper Mary held out, devouring its contents in a few seconds, and then, making an effort to be calm, read it again, more slowly.

Dear Gen,

You will probably have heard of the hobble I am in, and are no doubt worried half to death with not having heard from me. Well, it is worse, even then you have been told, for I am hurt, though not gravely. The thing is, I need money, quickly, for all I had was taken from me that evening, and I could not recover it in my haste. There is a fellow says he can get me to France, but he wants more than I can possibly raise, in the time. If you can bring old Lyle to sticking point do so, but don't delay. The fellow cannot wait above a day or two, and I must get away. If you come to the Cock, in the City, at four o'clock this afternoon, a girl will meet you and bring you to me. It's better you don't know where I am, for then you can't betray me. Don't fail me, Gen, I am counting on you.

George

Her brain in a whirl Genevieve screwed the paper tightly into a ball, and then, apparently reconsidering, spread it out and read it again. 'You will probably have heard of the hobble I am in.' What hobble? She had heard nothing at all, what could her brother possibly mean? She sat chewing her lip for a moment longer, and then, growing aware of Mary's concerned gaze she crumpled the note again and pushed it into the pocket of her wrap.

'I will get up,' she announced briskly, swinging her feet to the floor on the words. 'George is in trouble and I must speak to Miss Pinkerton.'

She left her room without putting on her slippers, leaving the maid to wonder just how much worse things were going to get before her mistress realised what a useless piece her brother was.

As she had expected she found Miss Pinkerton sitting up in bed with her chocolate, the morning's mail scattered about her on the covers, a slightly tattered and darned cap set askew upon her greying curls. She appeared somewhat startled by her young friend's appearance in her room, and Genevieve began to realise that a sudden demand for information about someone who should have been a perfect stranger to her might be productive of some suspicion in her hostess. She forced herself to talk for several minutes upon unexceptional topics before daring to approach the real object of her visit, namely, what was it that had been mentioned the evening before about the Honourable Frederick Winthrop. She had a notion, she explained, that it was something quite scandalous, but had forgotten quite what it was.

A half an hour later Genevieve returned to her room. She had discovered all she needed to know—but what a discovery! That her own brother should be little more than a thief, and a card-sharp into the bargain! It was almost unbelievable! Had she not had the care of him since they were children? How could he have turned so utterly from the road she had shown him?

Her thoughts continued in this vein for a few minutes longer, until it occurred to her, most unpleasantly, that any example she had shown her young brother would not be likely to convince him of the error of his present ways. She was, after all, little more than a thief herself. What should she expect from the brother who had watched her perform one deception after another, taking without a pang of conscience the money thus gained, until it must have seemed to the youthful George as merely his right. Sick at heart, Genevieve absently allowed Mary to assist her into her gown, finally forcing her thoughts into a consideration of George's present predicament, and how she was to rescue him. He had said he was hurt; no doubt an injury sustained in that dare-devil leap from the balcony. Her heart lurched as she thought of it, and she pressed one hand to her temple, causing Mary to inquire solicitously if she felt quite the thing. Genevieve started, and then with a smile said that she had the headache a very little, but that it would doubtless pass off when she took the air.

'The air, Miss Gen? On such a nasty, wet day? You'll not think of it, surely! Why, you'll catch your death.'

'Perhaps, but it would not signify greatly if I did, I think,' Genevieve answered despondently, turning her back for the maid to fasten her buttons.

'Now, Miss Gen,' Mary scolded, her nimble fingers busy, 'that's a wicked way to talk, and no mistake. Why, what your dear mother would think to hear you talk so I can't imagine, after she brought you into the world, too!'

Genevieve sighed. 'Oh, Mary! Whatever am I to do? You cannot conceive how much I wish for her now, and Papa, too.'

'Humph,' the maid said, turning her mistress around and peering somewhat sharply into her face. 'Well, I always swore I'd never interfere with what you and Master George got up to between you, and until now I've seen no cause. But I promised your mother I'd see you all right, and I'd be failing in my duty if I didn't say that you let that young man have too much of his own way. Takes advantage of you something terrible, he does, and if you try to tell me that this worriting you're doing ain't on his account, well, I shan't believe you.'

'Oh, Mary, whatever am I to do? He is in such a hobble, you can have no notion.'

'Well, that's where you're wrong, miss. His man, Collins, told me there have been some mighty queer folk looking for him, lately, which don't surprise me, I can tell you.'

'Well, he is in a sad case, and what I am to do about it I haven't the least notion. At least, I have, but it isn't what I want, at all.'

'Humph,' Mary said again, giving her mistress a shrewd glance. 'It's that plaguy fellow Lyle, I make no doubt. Well, I could have warned you, if I thought you'd have listened.'

'Warned me, Mary? What about?'

'About tangling with confirmed rakes, Miss Gen, that's what. Practised, they are, and this one more than most, at making young ladies fall head over ears in love with them. And if you try to tell me he hasn't succeeded, well, I just shan't believe you, that's all.'

Genevieve shook her head, her voice too choked for her to speak.

'And now, I suppose, the ungrateful varmint doesn't want anything to do with you!'

'Oh, Mary, if only that were true.' She sighed, and passed one hand across her eyes. 'He says he wants nothing more than to call me his wife. Could anything be more dreadful?'

'Well!' Mary exclaimed, shaking out her mistress's nightdress with some violence. 'If that don't beat all! There's a maggot in your brain, and no mistake. Here you are, mooning about like some love-sick calf over the fellow, and then you say there's nothing more dreadful than that he actually wants to marry you! Whatever are you waiting for, Miss Gen? Ain't it the answer to all your troubles? Don't try to tell me you've enjoyed your way of living, for I shan't believe you. Oh, I know, it suited you well enough in the beginning, you always was a wild creature, but I've seen plainly enough that you haven't cared for it this year or more. And it's no surprise, either, when by rights you should be settled, with a husband and family, not gallivanting all over the country like you do.'

Genevieve smiled, but said, 'Indeed, Mary, you don't understand. It's true, I feel for Sir Robert—something I did not know could be felt—but don't you see how impossible it would be? He thinks I'm some sort of French émigrée, not a hardened adventuress, and one, besides, who cheated his uncle out of two thousand pounds.'

'Well,' Mary remarked, guiding her charge to a stool and sitting her on it, 'I always did think it a trifle risky to tangle with two members of the same family, but it's too late, now, to cry over *that*. Tell him the truth, child, that's my advice. No doubt he'll cut up stiff—what can you expect?—no man likes to be taken for a ride, after all, but if he's worth anything at all he'll see what you really are, mark me.'

'If only it were so simple!' Genevieve exclaimed, sighing. 'If I thought he would forgive me, then everything would be different, but can't you see, Mary, how awful is this thing I have done? You said yourself, no man liked to be made game of—I should be lucky if he didn't immediately summon the constable. Then I should probably be transported, or some such thing, and how could I help my poor George then?'

'Poor George? Poor George? What the devil has he to say to anything, may I ask? You'll no doubt want to eat me for this, Miss Gen, but that boy deserves no more than he gets, and if he's in trouble, well, I make no doubt it was through some fault of his, not yours.' Catching up the hair-brush she began with some force to brush her mistress's hair.

'It isn't his fault!' Genevieve exclaimed hotly. 'It's mine, entirely. I gave him the example, after all, and now he's hurt, perhaps quite dreadfully, and forced to go into hiding. Oh, Mary, he talks of escaping to France.'

'Humph, in trouble with the law, is he? Well, I ain't surprised. It's my opinion he was responsible for Miss Pinkerton's snuff-box that there was all the fuss over, for he had been here that day, I know for a fact.'

'I fear you may be right. But what can I do? He's all the family I have, and don't try to tell me I'm not responsible for him, for I know I am. And now he needs money desperately, and the only way I can see to get it is to marry Sir Robert, and then I shall have to leave him and he'll hate me for ever.'

The last was on a wail, and to the maid's consternation her mistress leapt suddenly from the stool where she had been sitting to cast herself face downwards on the bed, regardless of the fate of her gown.

For some minutes Mary let her cry, sitting beside her on the bed, and stroking the golden curls as she had been used to do with a much younger Genevieve. After a while, however, when the tears showed no sign of stopping, she ceased her rhythmic strokes and said bracingly. 'Now then, Miss Gen, that ain't the least particle of use, as well you know. You'll make your eyes red and puffy, and then who will look at you? Come, sit up, and let me dry your face. Goodness knows what you've done to your dress, taking on in such a way.'

With an effort Genevieve sat up and glanced furtively at her maid. Her face was wet but neither puffed nor red, and Mary said briskly, 'There now. Come along, do, Miss Gen. I do believe it's stopped raining, and if you've to marry that Sir Robert then you'd better be ready when he comes for you, for no gentleman likes to be kept waiting, that I do know.'

Genevieve sniffed, but obeyed, standing passively while the woman arranged her gown afresh, fussing over the tiny creases her display of emotion had occasioned.

'There, Miss Gen, you'll do, I believe, but for heaven's sake wipe your cheeks. Watering-pots Gentleman hate so, you mark me, so it'll not do for him to see you with salt all over your face. Take this, and look sharp.'

Stretching out her hand Genevieve received the square of silk and dabbed obediently at her cheeks.

'Now then smile, Miss Gen, and see if you can't forget that plaguy brother of yours for just five minutes. There's no one more charming or beautiful than you, remember that, and if this fellow's worth anything at all he'll see it soon enough, mark me. Now smile.'

Genevieve obeyed, and the maid nodded sharply,

picking up her reticule and pushing it into Genevieve's limp grasp. 'You'll do well enough. Don't forget your warm wrap, Miss Gen, whatever you do, or that plaguy French accent of yours.' She shook her greying head. 'Turn in her grave, your poor mother would,' Mary muttered as her mistress left the room.

If Sir Robert had thought his love distracted the evening before he thought her desperate now, and the pathetic little smile she gave him as he handed her into his curricle would have been sufficient to melt a far sterner man than Sir Robert. He said nothing, however, merely inquiring politely after her health, and trusting that her headache of the evening before had quite disappeared.

'*Pardon*? Oh, yes, thank you, Sir Robert.' She gave a little laugh. 'Truly, m'sieur, you must forgive me. *Je regrette*, I was not myself last evening. If—if I was rude to you, I 'ope, m'sieur, that you will try to understand.'

'Dear child.' Sir Robert felt himself obliged to laugh. 'You were not rude, merely preoccupied with some trouble you have not told me of, I suspect.'

''Ow clever you are!' Genevieve exclaimed with a forced smile. 'But it is nothing, *je vous assure*.'

Sir Robert was silent for several minutes. Out of the corner of his eye he could see the young woman biting her lip, and noticed too that her hands were active among the folds of her wrap as though she did not know what they did. He was tooling his curricle very gently about the Park, but he thought she would not have noticed had he taken her to Brighton, or, worse, driven her down St James's Street. After a quarter of an hour, however, he decided it was time he broke her reverie, and he said accordingly with great gentleness, 'My dear Valentine, if there is something troubling you I wish you would tell me what it is. I am very broad-minded, you know. There is little that could shock me.'

She had started as he spoke and now turned huge, apprehensive eyes in his direction. 'No, no, there is nothing, *je vous assure*.' She fell silent again for a few moments and once more he began to hope until she turned to him again and said, 'Sir Robert, do you really wish to marry me?'

'Mlle Deneuve, I really do.'

'And—and you 'ave the special licence?'

He nodded. 'It is in my pocket this very instant. Should you care to examine it?'

'No. Oh no, no.' She hesitated a moment longer and then said with a quick smile, 'You do not mind being married, very soon?'

'Mademoiselle, I do not mind in the least. We may be married tomorrow if that is what you wish. No doubt some priest could be persuaded into it. We are both of age.'

'Tomorrow.' She seemed to give the matter her consideration. 'This is not too soon for you?'

He shook his head. 'All the arrangements had been made, mademoiselle. It is merely for you to name the day.'

The young lady took a breath. 'Very well. If you truly mean it and are not—um—*roasting* me, I think I should like it very much if we could be married tomorrow. Early,' she added as an afterthought.

Sir Robert bowed. 'Just as you wish, mademoiselle. I am entirely at your disposal. Do you wish for Miss Pinkerton to be present?'

'Mlle Pinkerton! Oh no, no. No,' she said utterly despondent, 'I think it should be quite private. You and I, *seulement*.'

'Unfortunately, charming though it would be, that will not be possible. It is necessary, you know, to have two witnesses, but if there is no one you wish to invite then I shall take it upon myself to provide them.'

'Witnesses!' The thought had plainly not occurred to Mlle Deneuve. 'Not your family!'

Sir Robert smiled slightly. 'You will soon discover, my dear, that there are very few members of my family that I have the slightest affection for, certainly not for those who would be available to attend.'

'Your brother?'

'My brother and stepmother. Have no fear. They shall know nothing whatever of the matter until it is announced in the *Gazette*.'

'Then who?'

Sir Robert considered. 'Two of my friends, two who will not take it upon themselves to spread the news about Town before we have time to escape.'

Genevieve nodded. 'They will think it very odd, *sans doute*.'

'It will be a nine-days' wonder, my dear. Don't worry. Something will soon occur to make everyone forget us.'

'If only that might be true. *Croyez vous*, do you think, m'sieur, that people will think it very bad?'

'I certainly hope not,' Sir Robert responded, smiling. 'There are many things a great deal worse.'

'Yes there are, *sans doute*.'

She fell silent once more, and they continued together without speaking for some little while until Sir Robert, with a covert glance in her direction, said diffidently, 'It occurs to me, mademoiselle, since you are, shall we say, embarrassed financially, that you might have need of some money before tomorrow. I do hope you would not hesitate to mention this if it were so.'

'Money?' Genevieve spoke dazedly.

'Yes. There are things, no doubt, that you will wish to buy. I should not like to think you were not able to do so.'

Genevieve shook her head. '*Vraiment*, m'sieur, that is very kind of you, but I shall manage I believe. I should not care to trouble you.'

Sir Robert contemplated her gravely for a moment, started to speak, and then apparently thought the better of whatever he had been about to say. After glancing at him inquiringly Genevieve sank back into thoughtfulness, and thus they continued until he had returned her to Brunswick Square.

CHAPTER
NINE

ON the morning of her wedding Genevieve awoke
heavy-eyed and far from refreshed. She had slept badly,
as was usual lately, but last night her dreams had taken
on a far more desperate quality. She had found George
flushed and feverish. The girl who had met her at the
Cock, in the City, had performed some hasty surgery
upon the injured leg, and when Genevieve arrived she
found her brother sitting up upon a hard truckle-bed, a
filthy blanket dragged up to his chin, his face flushed and
dark eyes sparkling with an unnatural brightness. He
greeted her with a laugh quite unlike his own, and as
Genevieve's eyes fell upon a dark, greasy bottle on the
floor beside him she was at no loss to account for this, at
least. The girl, a creature in a torn scarlet dress and with
hair of an improbable corn-yellow, had slouched in
behind her, and now stood leaning against the door-
jamb, her quick dark eyes rarely still.

'On the mop,' this lady remarked obscurely, jerking
her head at the bottle. Seeing Genevieve's bewildered
expression she added rather more intelligibly, 'Set his
leg, gave him the mop. Only way.'

'Oh George!' Genevieve exclaimed, understanding
enough. 'Have you broken your leg?'

He grinned at her. 'Stupid balcony. Twenty feet high,
more perhaps. Still, Nell took care of me, didn't you,

Nell? Set my leg like some cursed saw-bones.'

'Will you be able to walk, dearest? Is it very bad?'

He shrugged his shoulders beneath the blankets and grinned again. 'I dare say I shall have a limp, but that don't signify if only I can get away. Did you bring the money?'

Genevieve perched on the end of the grim little bed and surveyed him gravely. 'No, dearest, but I shall have it in a day or two, I promise.'

'A day or two! Shall I have to stay a day or two in this hole? I don't think I can bear it, Gen!'

His sister sighed. 'There's nothing else I can do. Sir Robert will give me the money, I know, but not for a day or two. Believe me, if there were any other way I would have found it.'

George shifted restlessly beneath the blanket and winced. 'Well, if it can't be helped it can't, though I'd as lief be away from here before the Runners find me, if it's all the same to you.'

'Of course, dearest! If only there were some way to help you sooner, but Sir Robert wouldn't—' She hesitated, and then shook her head. 'Dearest, I shall be as quick as I can, believe me. In a couple of days I shall come back, and then we may go away, to France, as you said. I believe it may be quite pleasant to be back in Paris.'

'I don't care where I am,' her brother replied, 'as long as I can get out of the country. This is the devil's own business, Gen.'

'I know, dearest, and it's all my fault, too.'

'Well, I don't know how you reason that, but I don't deny that if you'd given me the dibs when I asked for them I shouldn't have had to resort to such underhand dealings.'

Genevieve opened her mouth to protest, but then she apparently thought better of whatever she had been about to say, for she sighed, and fell to contemplating the bare floor-boards. 'If only there were something I could sell!' she exclaimed at last, rising and taking several hasty steps about the dark little room. 'But I have nothing of any value.' She glanced at him again and said, 'Just for a blanket, to keep you a little warmer.'

'Oh, I'm warm enough, thank you, Gen. In fact, I was going to ask you to open the window. It's like some cursed oven in here.'

Genevieve stared, but the girl in the doorway, in her usual terse style, said, 'Fever.'

'Oh dear! Has he—has he been like this very long?'

She shrugged. 'Stale drunk, 'e is, 'ow can I tell?'

'If only I could get a doctor to him!' Genevieve cried, wringing her hands and agitatedly pacing the floor.

'Now, Gen, don't even consider such a thing. Why, the fellow would have the Watch here in a minute. Leave me be, I'll be all right if only I can get away.'

'Well, I do hope so, dearest, indeed. Do you think you should be drinking quite so much? I'm sure it can't be doing the least good if you're not well.'

George eyed her with some indignation in his brilliant eyes. 'Lord, Gen, what the devil am I supposed to do? Have you the least notion how much a broken leg pains? I swear I fainted twice while Nell set the damn thing, and that with the balls of fire.'

'Balls of fire!' Genevieve exclaimed, her blue eyes staring.

'Brandy. Devilish rough. Ball of fire, best I could do.'

'Oh George!'

'Don't "Oh George" me! I can't bear it, as you well know. I tell you, Gen, if you'd had to put up with the half of what I have you wouldn't Oh George me in that ridiculous fashion.'

Genevieve did not answer, and after a moment George sank back upon the lumpy pillow and shut his eyes.

'You leave 'im be,' Nell advised her gruffly. 'You'll do no good with your breakteeth words, so 'ave done! Bring 'im the readies, and get the flash covey out of my way.'

'And so I will, just as soon as I am able.' She glanced at George again, but already sounds of sleep were emanating from his slumped form, so she turned to the girl again and said, 'Do look after him, won't you, until I return? He's little more than a child, you must see that.'

'No more than a mouth,' Nell responded obscurely. 'Now you be off, leave me and the flash cove be.'

Genevieve hesitated a moment longer, glanced at the slumbering form on the bed, and then turned upon her heel.

'Don't come back without the rolls of soft,' Nell advised her caustically from over the banisters. 'You and your breakteeth words!'

Her mind preoccupied by what she had seen Genevieve returned to find a note awaiting her in Brunswick Square. It was brief and to the point, but served to drive the last vestige of colour from her cheeks. Sir Robert, it would seem, had managed to make all the necessary arrangements, and if she would only present herself at St George's, Hanover Square, at eleven o'clock on the following morning he would undertake to see her properly wed. This letter made her tremble a very little, but she forced herself to think of George and his predicament, and pushed the piece of paper into her reticule with an air of determination. She had given very little thought to what she should wear on this momentous occasion, but when she reached her chamber she bade the waiting Mary to put out one of her better muslins as she was to be married the following morning.

'And you had better make sure your best black is pressed, Mary, for I shall need you to give me countenance.' Genevieve said casually, having decided that to go quite unattended to her wedding might not be quite what she would like.

'Humph,' this sour-faced female said gruffly. 'Tomorrow, is it? And a skimble-skamble business, too, by the sounds of it!'

'What can that possibly signify?' Genevieve demanded crossly, reluctantly submitting to her maid's ministrations. 'Since it must be, I had rather it were as quiet as possible. At least that way I may escape *some* notice.'

'Well, it's my opinion you've a maggot in your top-loft, Miss Gen, and no mistake! How your mother would take on if she only knew! I'm sure I never thought to see such a day!'

'I don't see that it can possibly make any difference,' Genevieve said, stepping absently from her gown. 'To be sure, I had much rather not have been obliged to marry Sir Robert, but it can't be helped, and I dare say he will divorce me just as soon as he realises.' She continued to stare in a preoccupied manner at the floor, and then considerably discomposed her maid by bursting into tears.

'Now then, Miss Gen, that's no way to carry on! You've made your decision, what need is there to cry over it?'

'None, Mary, none at all,' Genevieve said, her voice considerably muffled by the action of her handkerchief.

'Crack-brained, that's what it is. And if you ask me, that brother of yours needs a good talking to, and I can tell you, Miss Gen, I shan't scruple to give it to him when next I see him, nor won't Collins either, I dare say.'

'You're not to say a word to him, Mary,' Genevieve said, her tears ceasing miraculously. 'None of this is his fault, and besides, he is terribly hurt and can't help himself, so what else can I do?'

Mary sniffed, but did not condescend to answer.

Genevieve had been engaged to attend a ball that evening, but she excused herself, much to Miss Pinkerton's dismay, saying she had the headache and thought she would merely rest a little upon her bed. Since the event promised to be one of the season's successes Miss Pinkerton was more disturbed than she let her young charge see, particularly since it had been a matter of discussion and speculation between them for some weeks. She toyed with the idea of remaining at home herself, but since her dear Valentine was quite insistent that she go, pointing out that there was not the slightest need for both of them to miss the treat, she resolved to attend, but nevertheless decided to excuse herself early that the child might not be left too long alone.

Miss Christy, with no more than a modest cloak-bag, presented herself at the appropriate time at the doors of St George's Church, Hanover Square. There she found the bridegroom, with two friends in attendance, patiently awaiting her, but felt so very nervous, and indeed ill, that she could do no more than glance at his presumably radiant countenance as she entered the church. Everything went quite smoothly, no one being present to make any possible objection, and if the priest and Sir Robert's friends thought the whole affair decidedly strange, with the bride so nervous and distraught her responses were scarcely audible, none had the temerity to say so, and the whole affair passed off without a hitch.

It was only as she found herself ushered into a waiting carriage that Genevieve permitted herself to wonder where she was being taken, and whether it would be too far for her to return in time with the money for her brother. She glanced about her for Mary, but the maid seemed to have disappeared, and as the door was noiselessly shut upon them she turned to her new husband with wide, apprehensive eyes.

'Sir Robert, where is my maid? Is she not to travel with us?'

The gentleman smiled. 'She travels behind, my dear, do you mind? I thought it might be more pleasant if we could be alone. In fact, since we cannot possibly be in the slightest hurry it is quite possible she will be there before us. Do not concern yourself.'

'But where are we going? Is it very far?'

The gentleman shook his head. 'Near Bexley, merely. It is a delightful day, I suggest you settle yourself and enjoy the drive.'

Genevieve did as she was bid, quite relieved to discover that her new husband, so far from wanting to press his attentions upon his bride, was apparently quite content to do the same himself, and enjoy the scenery. He seemed, too, to think conversation unnecessary, a fact which did not occur to the new Lady Lyle until they stopped presently for luncheon, and she realised that neither of them had uttered a word for half an hour or more. Her agitation was still so great she thought she would not be able to swallow a morsel, but when the selection of cold meats was presented to her she suddenly discovered herself to be ravenous, a fact she was soon able to account for by remembering she had had no breakfast. Sir Robert, too, was able to partake heartily, seemingly quite unconcerned by his bride's sudden lack of conversation, or the fits of preoccupation which would cause her to sit abstractedly for several minutes together, her fork suspended midway between her plate and her mouth. It was only as they neared their destination that it occurred to Genevieve that some curiosity about her new home might be expected and she roused herself sufficiently to inquire of Sir Robert where they were going.

'Dearing,' he responded, smiling very slightly.

'Oh.' Genevieve thought for a moment and then said, 'That is your family 'ome?'

Sir Robert nodded. 'I trust you will not be too disappointed. I'm afraid it is considered by some to be perfectly hideous, but I must admit to being quite fond of it.'

'Oh,' Genevieve said again, and then apparently thinking some further interest to be required asked, 'Do you 'ave a great many servants?'

'Enough, I hope, for our needs, but you must feel free to hire just as many as you feel to be necessary. It is your home, after all, from now on.'

Genevieve stared at him. It was a thought that had not previously occurred to her and one which, unaccountably, filled her with an even greater sense of desolation. She was forced to take a very strong hold upon her emotions that she should not burst ridiculously into tears. The feeling grew rather than abated, so that when the carriage finally swept through an impressive gateway and began winding its way up a finely gravelled drive she felt she could almost not bear to look from the window as her 'home' came into view. Curiosity prevailed, however, and she found herself staring at a large, sprawling edifice that might once have been called beautiful, but which had been so added to and modified over the years that it now lacked any form or design. There was, however, Genevieve decided shortly, something particularly appealing about its motley collection of roofs and windows, something so utterly unpretentious and homely, that Genevieve felt she could have been happy there. No guide-book to Kent would have described it as worth a visit; no ambitious matron sigh and say that of such a noble pile her dearest Emily or Jane might have been mistress. This was a home, something to be lived in rather than admired, and for a moment Genevieve almost found herself wondering whether she could consign George to the rightabout and stay in Kent.

It was but a momentary aberration. The carriage crunched to a halt outside the wide doors, footmen appeared to open the carriage door, she heard herself addressed as 'My Lady', and found herself gently pressured to descend. Reality returned in a moment. She was an adventuress; such was the stuff of dreams and not for her. Her style of life had been decided early, she could not change it now. Long practice came to her aid. As the footman bowed her from the carriage she was able to smile and thank him, able, even, to look with interest as she passed between the wide doors into the panelled hall, and to inquire of her husband when it had been built.

As he had foretold, Mary had arrived somewhat in advance of them and was to be found now in the act of laying out her mistress's evening-gown.

'Though why I'm bothering I don't know, for I've no doubt you don't mean to stay,' this good female grumbled, smoothing the small creases from the fine muslin.

'I shall stay tonight,' Genevieve answered, abstractedly seating herself at the dressing-table and removing the pins from her hair.

'To think we might have been set for life if it weren't for that good-for-nothing brother of yours,' Mary continued, moving to her mistress and taking the brush from her grasp. 'It grieves me, Miss Gen, I don't deny it. Why don't you tell 'im? What have you got to lose, after all? Chances are he'll stick by you. He's married you, after all, and what gentleman wants to be made to look a fool by his wife?'

'You don't know what you're saying, Mary,' Genevieve said dully, sinking a little on her stool. 'He would be quite deadfully angry, I make no doubt, and besides, he could always hand me to a magistrate for what I did to his uncle.'

'Pooh!' said Mary roundly, inflicting her mistress's hair with several brisk stokes. 'What need to tell him that? The chances are he'd never find out.'

'Of course he would, in time, and only think how much worse it would appear after a few months, or even years. Besides,' she added dismally, 'I don't believe I could deceive him in a such a way.'

'It's demented you are, Miss Gen, and no mistake! Blow me if I ever thought to hear such skimble-skamble reasoning from you. You can't deny that you're head over ears in love with the fellow, so what ails you, for the Lord's sake? What have you got to lose? Tell him everything, that's my advice, and mark me if 'e don't forgive you it all.'

'Oh, Mary!' Genevieve wailed, covering her face with her hands, 'if only I could: I would risk it, I know, if it were only me, but what about George? Whatever will he think if I tell him I only married him so that he could get George away from those dreadful Runners? Why, he might even refuse to give me the money, and then what should I do? George would be taken, for sure.'

'Your brain's addled,' Mary said bluntly. 'Stupid, I call it. Can't you think of anyone but that scape-grace brother of yours for two minutes together? I dare say he'd manage if you didn't get the money, for he's a survivor, make no mistake about it. And I don't doubt that it would do him a great deal of good to be obliged to take care of himself for a change. You've protected him too long, Miss Gen, and that's the truth.'

Genevieve said nothing. She continued to stare without seeing at her reflection in the glass, and Mary, after waiting in vain for an answer, sniffed, and began pinning up her mistress's hair.

She did not stop thinking, however. Throughout the time it took her to prepare her mistress for dinner her brain, rarely idle, was particularly active, and she was so quiet that Genevieve, had she had the inclination, might have thought something severely amiss with her usually garrulous maid. She did not, however, merely thanking her maid in an absent voice and leaving the room without her reticule.

For some minutes Mary continued in her abstraction. Whilst mechanically tidying her mistress's discarded clothes she was daring to form the boldest of plans, and, lest her courage fail her, resolved to put it into action without delay. Her mistress's new dressing-room adjoined Sir Robert's, and she had heard the low rumble of male voices which signified the presence of the master and his man. Consequently, when she felt her courage to be high enough she knocked smartly on the adjoining door and waited to be admitted.

It was the master's man, Denby, who opened the door, a look of patent disapproval upon his thin face when he saw who stood there.

'I was wishful for a word with the master,' Mary said

boldly, raising her chin a little in the face of such disdain.

'What can you possibly have to say to the master?' Denby demanded, sneering very slightly at such obvious low-breeding. 'He's getting ready for dinner, and has no time to waste on the likes of you.'

'That's not for you to say,' Mary retorted, bridling at such high-handed treatment. 'What I have to discuss with Sir Robert concerns him alone, and is, besides, of some importance.'

'"Importance." Who to, may I ask? Not the master, that's certain.'

'It's little enough you know, then,' Mary answered crossly, 'and I tell you to your head, Mr Denby, that your master will be mighty displeased if he finds out you've stopped me.'

Denby hesitated. He felt his authority to be severely endangered by such behaviour, but nevertheless, if what this strange female had to communicate was really so important it would go ill with him if he prevented her. Consequently he eyed the creature down the length of his Roman nose and said loftily, 'Wait here, I will see if the master can spare you a few seconds.'

The door was shut in her face. Affronted, Mary nevertheless did not allow herself to be put out by such treatment. She had received a great deal worse in the past, and besides, what she had to say to Sir Robert was a great deal too important for it to bother her unduly.

In a few minutes the door opened again. Mary steeled herself to face another attack from the pestilential Denby, and was consequently quite put out when she found herself staring up into Sir Robert's stern features.

'You wanted to speak to me? I do trust it is as important as you say, for you must know I am already late for dinner.'

'Oh sir, indeed it is important, desperately so. Only give me a moment or two, that's all I ask.'

'Very well.' Sir Robert spoke briskly, and then, with a glance over his shoulder at the hovering servant, entered his wife's dressing-room and firmly shut the door. 'Now, what is it?'

Mary hesitated. It was one thing, she now discovered, to have rehearsed her speech a dozen times to herself, and quite another to deliver it when the recipient was standing so severely over her, itching with impatience, and clearly wishing her to have done. She took a breath, however, recollecting that she had very little to lose, and began, 'It concerns my mistress, sir.'

'Indeed?' Sir Robert's tone remained impatient, but Mary, far from stupid, thought she detected a slight sharpening of interest in the hard grey eyes.

'Sir, you must know that my mistress is vastly unhappy.'

'Indeed, I was aware of no such thing. I am not the cause, I trust.'

'Oh no! That is, yes, but it's not your fault. Oh dear! When I thought of this it all seemed so simple. Now I hardly know where to start.'

Sir Robert contemplated her for a moment or two in silence, and then said in a much gentler tone, 'Start at the beginning, if you please. You will find me an excellent listener.'

Nearly half an hour later Mary, having told her mistress's life-story, paused for breath, and looked in some anxiety at Sir Robert. 'Oh dear,' she said agitatedly, 'I do hope I have not made the most terrible mistake.'

For a moment Sir Robert did not answer. There was an expression on his face Mary did not know how to interpret, and the dreadful fear that he might hand her beloved mistress to the Authorities loomed large. Then he turned, and smiled slightly. 'Mary, I am very grateful to you. You have taken a great weight from my shoulders.'

'You—you don't mind?'

Sir Robert shrugged. 'I dare say I should, very much, except, you see, your mistress never deceived me. I knew what she was about from the first.'

'You *knew*?'

He nodded. 'Some while ago I received a letter from a relation of mine, Claudius Lyle, telling me he was about to be married. This seemed so extraordinary that I could not resist paying him a visit, only to discover, as you know, that his young lady had fled. As you may imagine, I was quite incensed, and promised my uncle that I would do all in my power to bring the young lady to the fate she so evidently deserved. To achieve this I offered myself as bait, intending, I suppose, to pay her back in her own coin. What I could not have anticipated was that I would succumb, as so many before me, to Miss Christy's plentiful charms. Ridiculous, isn't it?' He laughed wryly. 'And now you tell me that Miss Christy is not quite as indifferent to me as she would have me believe. Can you wonder that you see me so very relieved?'

Mary shook her head slowly. 'No, sir, but 'tis a pretty coil, and no mistake. She means to leave you, you must know, and go back to France with that plaguy brother of hers.'

Sir Robert frowned. 'And is that what she really wants?'

'Lord, sir, I don't know. It's my view she blames herself for the hobble he's in, though how she reasons that I can't imagine. He always was a worthless young

man, I've told her so more times than I can count, not
that she's ever listened to me.'

'And to save this worthless young man she means to
sacrifice herself, and me as well. As you say, it's a pretty
coil.'

'Aye, sir, and if you can solve it, well, you've a good
head on your shoulders, that's all I can say.'

Sir Robert smiled. 'I'll solve it, though I must admit,
just how presently eludes me. However, you may rest
easy. I do not mean to let my wife go as easily, of that you
may be sure.'

Mary sighed. 'Thank you, sir. You don't know what a
relief it is for me to hear you say so. Fair flummoxed me,
it has, to find a way out of this mess.'

CHAPTER
TEN

ON the morning of Genevieve's wedding Miss Pinkerton
had overslept. Although she had made a considerable
effort to be home betimes the previous evening, it had
been nearly two o'clock before she had finally extin-
guished her candle and pulled the covers beneath her
chin. Genevieve had been sleeping soundly, so she had
deduced that whatever had ailed the child earlier in the
day had not been sufficiently troublesome to rob her of
sleep. Consequently it was with a heart considerably
lighter that she sought her own couch, sleeping undis-
turbed well into the following day, and waking with no
sense at all of what had recently occurred. The first
intimation she received of Genevieve's departure came
when her maid, Milly, peered cautiously round the door
to see if her mistress were awake. Since Miss Pinkerton
was lying on her back in earnest contemplation of the
ceiling she felt emboldened to enter, presenting her
mistress with the morning's mail. It was on the top of this
pile that she had laid a neatly addressed envelope, one
which had not been delivered, as had the rest, through
the post, but which had been discovered early reposing
upon the hall-table. Miss Pinkerton raised her brows. It
was not a hand she recognised, and she slit it open with a
feeling of pleasurable anticipation. Some minutes later
Milly returned, bearing this time her mistress's mug of

chocolate, and was startled to discover this good woman already out of her bed, in the act of fastening her wrap somewhat hastily about her shoulders. The mug was ignored, Miss Pinkerton leaving the room as Milly entered it and hurrying along the passage to the guest-chamber. Since she had some notion of what had occurred Milly was not entirely surprised by this, for it had been her opinion all along that her mistress had been sadly taken-in by the young person she had chosen to favour in so particular a manner. What she was not prepared for, however, was her mistress's almost instantaneous return, and a command that she should set out her grey pelisse at once as she was going out.

Contrary to Milly's expectation Miss Pinkerton did not feel herself to have been grossly deceived by Mlle Deneuve. It was plain to her after a very little contemplation what must have occurred, and she did not intend to let it pass unnoticed. Mlle Deneuve had obviously seen subjected to one her wretched brother's diatribes, which affected her so deeply that she had decided to pack up her belongings at once and leave. How well could Selina Pinkerton imagine the scene! How Henry had managed it she could not be sure but manage it he must have, for why else would her dear Valentine leave so quickly, and with no real explanation? It explained, too, the poor child's preoccupation of late; she must have been considering her departure for quite some time. Well, Henry must not be permitted to get away with such behaviour. He had interfered in her life quite enough already and if he thought he could intimidate the child into running away he had underestimated his sister. Returning to her room she took up Valentine's letter again and perused it thoughtfully. Of course, the dear child had given no hint, talking in the vaguest terms of being obliged to go away, and expressing her great distress at being unable to say goodbye. It was only Too Plain, and Miss Pinkerton suddenly found herself feeling very angry indeed, an emotion quite uncommon in this gentle spinster. Turning to her wide-eyed maid she bade her briskly to 'look sharp' as she intended going out and had not the least moment to waste. Her curiosity burning the girl did as she was bid, only wishing she might know just who had been responsible for putting her usually gentle mistress into such a taking.

Within a half-hour Miss Pinkerton was seated in her carriage, quite calm, but with her anger not one jot abated. She had no doubt of her brother's guilt; it would be just like him, she thought, to try some underhand method of spoiling her pleasure.

The butler who admitted her to her brother's house was in some doubt about his master's availability, and Miss Pinkerton remembered, with some scorn, that her brother rarely left his chamber before noon. It was a habit she had always deplored: now it merely served to strengthen her in her resolve.

'Pray inform my brother that I am here,' she said, removing her gloves and laying them on the hall-table. 'I have no doubt but that he will not wish to see me, so you may tell him that I have every intention of waiting.'

The butler bowed, and was obliged to keep his inevitable curiosity under control.

The Earl of Maland was indeed sorely put out by the information that his sister was below, with, apparently, no intention of being fobbed off. She had, he well knew, a curiously stubborn streak, he had noticed it with chagrin on more than one occasion when his usually tractable relation had, for some unaccountable reason, dug in her heels over some apparently trivial matter.

Witness that French female! Henry still smarted from his sister's obstinacy in that affair, and as he allowed his valet to ease him into his coat began to wonder how forgiving he should be if his sister had come to ask for his aid. He decided he should be magnanimous. He was her only source of assistance, after all, and if she were sufficiently repentant, why, he saw no reason at all why he should not forgive her. After a suitable period of reflection, of course. Accordingly he descended the stairs with more than his usual air of consequence, the sternness of his expression nicely tempered by understanding.

His sister had been growing impatient. It was some time, now, since she had had the least sympathy with her brother's foibles, and being kept waiting nearly three quarters of an hour while he arranged his cravat was not what she liked. When he opened the door in his regal manner and stood grimly before her she knew none of the remorse he would have expected, merely a growing sense of irritation and injustice.

'Well, Selina?' the Earl began, taking his watch from his pocket and glancing at it. 'I wish you would tell me what is so urgent! I have an engagement!'

Miss Pinkerton had not been waiting nearly an hour to be brushed off. She stood up, and regarded her brother firmly in the eye. 'I have come, Henry,' she said, 'for an explanation.'

'An explanation?' The Earl was, for once, at a loss.

'I wish to know, Henry,' Miss Pinkerton said, 'what you mean by frightening Valentine.'

'Frightening Valentine?' the Earl repeated, goggling slightly.

'Yes, Henry. Please do not attempt to deny it for I know perfectly well that it was you.'

'Indeed, Selina, I have not the slightest idea what you are talking about.'

'Don't fence with me, please! Who else could it have been? What I want to know is, did she tell you where she might go? I presume you gave her money, Henry, at least!'

The Earl of Maland stared at his sister, his brain slowly reaching some understanding of what she was saying. 'Am I to conclude, Selina, that that French hussy has abandoned you?'

The Honourable Miss Selina Pinkerton drew herself up. She was not unimpressive. 'She has left me, yes, as you well know. I wonder you have the impudence to try to bluster your way out of it.'

'Bluster? *Bluster*?' The Earl was considerably wounded by this method of attack. 'I do not bluster, Selina. If that—female had left you, well, I am sorry for you, but at least you are undeceived at last.'

'Really, Henry, this is too bad of you! Why do you persist in asserting it was not your doing?'

'*My* doing? Are you intimating, Selina, that you think I was the cause of the wretched woman's departure?'

'Certainly I am.'

'Well,' the Earl exclaimed, growing red in the face, 'if that don't beat all! Really, Selina, I don't know what's come over you lately. It ain't enough for you to fill your house with unknown foreign females, you actually accuse your only brother of doing his best to free you of her. Not but what it wouldn't have been a bad idea, but I assure you, it was no work of mine. Take my word for it, if she's left you it's for reasons of her own. I would suggest you have Milly check the silver.'

'Valentine was not that sort of girl,' Miss Pinkerton asserted warmly, but nevertheless a look of doubt crossed her face. 'Am I to take it, Henry, that you know nothing of this business?'

'Most certainly you are. Really, sister, do you honestly think that if I had been instrumental in the matter I would have denied it? I dare say I should have been vastly pleased with myself.'

Miss Pinkerton was silent for a moment and then said grudgingly, 'Well, you probably would. I never knew anyone who more delighted in spoiling sport than you, Henry Pinkerton.'

The Earl of Maland preserved his temper with an effort. It was typical of Selina, he thought, to try to reduce him to schoolroom status. He should have permitted her to become a governess after all. No doubt she would have been quite excellent. He raised his chins a little and said haughtily, 'If that is all you have to say, Selina, I shall bid you good morning. I have wasted a great deal too much time on this business already. You should have believed me when I told you I had washed my hands of this whole affair, but I hope I am not a vengeful man. We may continue as before, no doubt, now this unfortunate matter is at an end.'

Miss Pinkerton was silent. She wished, more than ever, that she could tell her unsufferable brother that she wished no longer to be obliged to him for the slightest thing, but she knew this was impossible so she held her peace, watching in silence while her brother moved, his corsets creaking, to pull the bell-rope.

'I trust, Selina,' he was saying, 'that this unfortunate business will prove salutary. I hope I am not one to delight in ignoble triumph, but you will recollect, I am sure, that I told you no good could come of such an association. Why, you knew nothing at all of the girl.' Having given the rope a vigorous tug he turned back to

face his sister, beginning, at last, to enjoy himself. His
pleasure, however, was short-lived. Miss Pinkerton,
taking advantage of her brother's turned back, had
quitted the room, and in a moment the Earl heard his
front door open and gently close.

Feeling considerably disturbed Miss Pinkerton had
allowed herself to be handed back into her carriage. She
had no doubt that, unpleasant though it was, Henry
spoke the truth. It would be impossible, she knew well,
for him to remain silent about what must have been a
considerable triumph on his part, and she was therefore
obliged to look elsewhere for enlightenment. Her reflec-
tions were now becoming uneasy. Had she, perhaps,
been too hasty in accepting a total stranger into her
home? Was the girl, after all, nothing but a clever fraud?
Miss Pinkerton could not believe it. The child had
received very little but her keep; the only present she
had allowed Miss Pinkerton to bestow upon her had
been the zephyr shawl, something that good lady had
never regretted once she had seen how becoming it had
looked. She forced herself to go back over their acquaintance, but there was no occasion that she could
think of—it was at this point that a most unpleasant
sensation gripped her. There was the affair of the snuff-
box; it had been a pretty piece, old and valuable now,
that had belonged to her father and was treasured by her
on that score alone. When she had discovered its absence Miss Pinkerton had been quite considerably distressed, particularly when the minutest search had failed
to uncover it. Surely Valentine could not have been
responsible for that? Surely, if in a moment of weakness
she had taken it, she could not have retained it once she
had seen her hostess's distress? But Miss Pinkerton
would not be easy. The thing had vanished so totally

without trace, and no one could recall that any stranger had been to the house who might at any time have pocketed it. The recollection was indeed an unhappy one, and Miss Pinkerton resolved, although with distaste, to check her possessions when she reached home.

A sudden silence around her, followed by the protesting of ancient springs as her coachman descended from his box, told her that they had arrived, and in a moment Thomas's wrinkled face appeared at the carriage window. The door opened and the steps were let down; Miss Pinkerton reached her front door at the same instant as a gentleman, one who doffed his hat and spoke to her. Miss Pinkerton turned. She had been so engrossed by her thoughts that she had failed to see him approach, and it was in some bewilderment that she looked up into the handsome face. Then she smiled.

'Why, Mr Lyle, how pleasant! Have you come to see Valentine?'

Joseph Lyle smiled. 'Indeed I have, Miss Pinkerton. She is at home?'

A denial was on Miss Pinkerton's lips, but then she hesitated. Valentine had gone driving with Mr Lyle on one occasion, and although Miss Pinkerton could not believe her to have been vastly taken by him it was yet possible that something might have been let slip. Accordingly she smiled and said, 'I'm afraid she isn't, Mr Lyle, but perhaps you would care to come inside in any case? I'm sure she will be most sorry to have missed you.'

Lyle would have refused. It was not his intention to spend the morning in idle conversation with a penniless spinster, but the door before him had now opened and he found himself ushered inside in a manner too persuasive to resist. In a moment he had been conducted upstairs to the little drawing-room and was being offered a glass of Madeira wine.

'I am sure Valentine will be *most* sorry to have missed you,' Miss Pinkerton was saying, hovering over him while he tasted the wine. 'I know how much she enjoyed her drive with you, Mr Lyle.'

Joseph expressed his gratification.

'Unfortunately I have to tell you that I have no idea at all when she will return.' Miss Pinkerton seated herself and took a sip of madeira. 'I have to admit, Mr Lyle, that Valentine is no longer with me.'

'Indeed!' Mr Lyle also sipped at the madeira, no longer regretting the impulse that had led him to Brunswick Square that morning.

Miss Pinkerton nodded. 'You are a man of discretion, Mr Lyle, I am sure. The truth of the matter is she has left me, and gone I know not where. It is very distressing.'

'Miss Pinkerton, I am truly sorry. Can it be that you have been deceived?'

'I hope not, indeed, though I must admit it does begin to look as though—Mr Lyle, when you took Valentine for that drive, did she say anything to you that might indicate she was not perfectly happy?'

He frowned for a moment, and took a reflective sip at his wine. 'No, Miss Pinkerton, I don't believe she did. In fact, I believe Mlle Deneuve spoke only of her great sense of obligation to you for your kindness. She said nothing at all of being obliged to leave us so soon.'

'Oh dear!' Miss Pinkerton sounded quite distracted. 'I so hoped she might have said something to you.'

Lyle shook his head. 'But you must remember, Miss Pinkerton, that we had only a very brief relationship. My brother, you must know, is far more likely than myself to have been the recipient of any confidence.'

'Do you think so?' Miss Pinkerton seemed doubtful. 'Indeed, Mr Lyle, I wonder if that is the case. Their friendship seemed so very casual.'

'No doubt you are right,' he conceded, bowing. 'I trust some news may be had of Mlle Deneuve soon, however.' He rose, and brushed his cream-coloured pantaloons. 'To be deceived is always unpleasant, Miss Pinkerton; it is to be hoped a harmless explanation may be had in time.'

'Oh, I hope so, indeed. Valentine was indeed such a charming girl, I really cannot believe—Oh, Mr Lyle, are you leaving so soon?'

'I'm afraid I must. I merely came to ask Mlle Deneuve to drive out with me. I must not, you know, keep my chestnuts standing too long. There is quite a breeze.'

'Of course, Mr Lyle, I quite understand.' Now that he was leaving Miss Pinkerton barely heard what he said.

Gaining the street again Mr Lyle swung himself into his curricle and gave the office to his groom. It was with considerable satisfaction that he directed his animals towards the park reflecting that his plan had succeeded a great deal better than he could have hoped. He had no conception that Mlle Deneuve, or whatever her name might be, would be so easily deflected from his brother, for he could have no doubt that her sudden disappearance had been the happy results of his own threats. It was all so very satisfactory! To have succeeded with so very little effort was really quite gratifying; he had supposed it would have taken a number of subsequent visits to persuade the harpy of the necessity of withdrawal, and indeed, that had been the very purpose of his visit that day. Reflecting that a turn in the Park would be extremely agreeable in any event he swung the curricle in at the Grosvenor Gate and began to tool it gently along the carriage-way.

The day was fine and spring-like, encouraging many persons to take the air. The paths were quite thronged with walkers, and Mr Lyle idly cast his eye along their ranks for any acquaintance. It was while he was un-ashamedly ogling one of the latest beauties and wondering whether to ask her into his curricle that he heard himself hailed and turned rather grudgingly to see a young man waving on the path. He sighed, and drew his animals to a halt. On any other occasion he would have been pleased to see Mr Wytham; he had at that moment however, decided that the fair Miss Debenham was worthy of his attention. Nevertheless he signed to his friend, and in a moment the young man had swung himself into the carriage to replace the groom and they were moving again.

'Now then, Joseph,' he said smiling, 'you would do well to look elsewhere than the lovely Miss Debenham. It's rumoured she and Wrexham are making a match of it.'

'Wrexham!' Joseph sounded more than usually put out by this information. 'What the devil does he want with her? More blunt than he knows what to do with already! He should leave the heiress for the rest of us.'

'Well, I can't say I don't agree with you, Jo. It's devilish hard, I must admit. Such a dashed fine female, too. It ain't so often you see money and beauty. Do you know, I'd decided to offer for her myself, that cursed aunt of mine seeming no nearer the grave, but I dare say I'd be wasting my time. No doubt it's been the title all along.'

'Hardly a doubt of it, I should think,' Joseph said dryly, the idea wrankling. 'If that cursed brother of mine would only die I could offer one myself.'

'But you'd only be a baronet, wouldn't you, Joseph. And besides, if what Corky tells me is true there's precious little chance of it now in any event.'

'Corky?' Joseph repeated irritably. 'What does he know of the matter?'

Mr Wytham smiled. 'Why, Joseph, can it be you hadn't heard? The word is it's a match between your brother and the mademoiselle.'

For once Joseph was moved to smile. 'Unlikely, Wytham. Why, I had it from the Pinkerton myself that Mlle Deneuve has seen fit to remove from Town.'

Mr Wytham whistled. 'Has she, indeed! There might be some truth in the tale after all.'

Mr Lyle was just then engaged in a complicated manoeuvre between a stationary tilbury and a slow-moving landaulet but he found time to glance at his companion and say testily, 'What tale, Wytham? Is there something I haven't heard?'

'It would seem so, indeed, Jo,' Mr Wytham replied, enjoying himself.

Lyle ground his teeth. 'Then I wish to hell you'd tell me what it is, and without roundaboutation, if you please.'

Mr Wytham smiled and examined his nails with some care. 'Well, it might be true, or it might not, you know what Corky is. Nevertheless, it's a rum tale and no mistake.' He glanced at his companion for his reaction and saw him preserving his temper with some difficulty. 'Well, as I said, it might be true or it might not. Thing is, Corky said he met Kavanagh this morning, rigged out like some bridegroom. Commented on it, for it ain't like Kavanagh to prance about like some dashed dandy, leastways not at twelve o'clock in the morning, which is when it was. "Oh," says Kavanagh, "you ain't far wrong. I'm not supposed to say," he says, "but it'll be all over Town in a day or two in any event. Been to a wedding. Lyle's wedding. He's married the Mademoiselle."' Mr Wytham paused, and glanced again at his companion. 'There! What do you think of that, Jo? Any truth in it? It's a strange tale to put about if there ain't, and you must admit, they've been wondrous great these past few weeks. Taking bets on it, at White's.'

Mr Lyle did not answer. He had gone, Mr Wytham noticed curiously, a peculiar grey colour, and he wondered if the fellow were about to have a seizure of some kind. Since he was driving his greys rather harder than was proper in the park he sincerely hoped this was not the case, and felt moved enough to say, with some uneasiness, 'I say, Joseph, are you all right? You missed that landau by a bare inch!'

'An inch is sufficient, I believe,' Mr Lyle replied caustically, not taking his eyes from the road, 'and if you value your skin you will keep quiet.'

For a few minutes Mr Wytham did as he was bid, but when the curricle swung through the gate with the sharp sound of scraping wood he was unable to stop himself from crying out, and grasping ineffectually at the side of the carriage.

'Be quiet, damn you,' Lyle exclaimed, his gaze fixed upon the road. 'It's no more than a scratch!'

'Maybe, but—I say, do slow down, Lyle, will you! They're all looking at us, and if you gave that coach a quarter of an inch I'm a madman.'

Lyle did not respond, being engaged now in weaving his way between the motley collection of carriages that littered the streets. With a shudder Mr Wytham closed his eyes and entrusted himself to fate.

They reached Berkeley Square in a very few minutes, and without incurring the accident that Mr Wytham had at one time considered inevitable. With a word to his groom Mr Lyle sprang from the carriage and ignored Mr Wytham altogether, running up the steps to his brother's house and pounding on the door. For a minute or two Mr Wytham sat still, but when the door opened and Lyle disappeared inside he sighed, and eased himself down to the pavement.

Joseph's demand to see his brother had produced a shake of the butler's greying head. The master, it would seem, had departed for Dearing earlier that day, and the butler was not in any expectation of his early return. Joseph Lyle swore.

'However, sir,' the butler continued, looking a little anxious, 'my master's great-uncle, Mr Claudius, might be found in the green drawing-room.'

Joseph had turned to the door with an oath, but at this information he hesitated, and swung back to the butler. 'Old Claudius? What's he doing here?'

'Indeed, sir,' Wareing responded, 'I have no notion. All I can say, sir, is that as far as I know the gentleman was not expected. At least, sir, *I* was not informed.'

'I see.' Joseph frowned momentarily. 'He has arrived, you say, since my brother's departure? He expected to find him here?'

'Indeed, sir, that would seem to be the case. And if I might be so bold, the gentleman seemed exceedingly put out, having travelled with the express purpose of having urgent conversation with my master, not to find him at home.'

Joseph was silent. There was more to this, he decided, than might at first seem possible. 'Where is my uncle now?'

'The green drawing-room, sir. Should I conduct you?'

'No, Wareing, I'll find my own way.' As he spoke Lyle was running up the stairs, and in a moment had reached the landing, and the drawing-room door.

His great-uncle stood at the window, a grim expression on his tired face. At the sound of the door he turned quickly, but seeing his younger grand-nephew grunted, and turned back to his contemplation of the street. 'So that's your rig, is it, Joseph? Should have known as much.' He glanced at his young relative and grimaced. 'You're becoming a dashed dandy, if you ask me. What the devil do you call that neckcloth?'

'A Mailcoach, sir.' Joseph spoke mechanically.

'Mailcoach, eh? Dashed stupid affair. How the devil are you supposed to turn your head, tell me that!'

'Sir, I have not come here to talk of cravats. Have you seen my brother?'

'The devil I have!' Claudius responded grimly, lowering at his grand-nephew from beneath fearsome eyebrows. 'And I journeyed all the way from Bedfordshire to speak to the fellow!'

'Then you know nothing of his whereabouts.'

'Nothing at all. Don't tell me he's given you the slip as well.'

'Not exactly. Wareing tells me he's at Dearing.'

'Humph. He may well be. No doubt he had word of my coming.'

Lyle frowned. 'Are you saying, sir, that my brother might have left London to avoid seeing you? I find that hard to believe.'

'Nevertheless, it's the truth.'

'But why should he wish to do that?' Lyle persisted. 'It ain't exactly like my brother to turn craven.'

'No, it ain't. And it ain't like Robert to deceive his old

uncle, yet that's what he's done.'

'Deceived you, sir?' Lyle queried, momentarily diverted. 'In what way?'

Claudius frowned. 'Never you mind. The thing is, I asked him to perform some commission for me and he hasn't done it.'

Lyle laughed. 'Well, sir, nothing would surprise me today. The latest on it, I would have you know, is that my brother has seen fit to marry some dashed adventuress. I came here to discover the truth of it, but it would seem we are both to be disappointed.'

His great-uncle gave a low growl. '*Married*, you say? You're telling me the fool's gone and married the wench?'

Joseph stared. His uncle, it would seem, knew something of the affair. 'That's what I heard, although I cannot guarantee its truth. Why, sir? Have you heard something in Bedfordshire?'

Claudius grunted. 'Didn't believe it. Wouldn't believe it. Not like Robert to serve an old man such a backhanded turn.'

'I wish, sir,' Joseph said, 'that you would tell me what this is all about.'

Claudius glowered at him for a moment and then said, 'Wench I was going to marry. She ran off with my money, and I sent Robert to bring her back. Friend of mine, General Courtenay, wrote to me. Said it was all over Town that Robert was making a cake of himself over some cursed female, French-woman, he said. Didn't take me long to reason what had happened.'

'Let me understand you sir. Are you telling me that it was Mlle Deneuve you were engaged to?'

The old man nodded. 'And now he's married her, you say. Robert!'

'You say that Robert followed her to London with the express purpose of bringing her before the Justices?' Joseph spoke strangely, but the old man appeared not to notice.

'Isn't that what I've just told you?' he snapped irritably, casting his grand-nephew a look of intense dislike. 'Couldn't think what was taking the fellow so long. Should have known.' He sighed, and shook his head. 'Should feel sorry for the boy, I suppose. There's no doubt but that she'll take him for a ride.'

'Could it be, sir,' Joseph suggested dryly, 'that she has decided her wandering days are over? Robert is, as we all know, a baronet.'

'I ain't forgotten that, Joseph, and I make sure you haven't!' He looked at Joseph, more searchingly this time, and of a sudden cackled. 'Do you know, the one comfort to me in this danged business is that the chances are she'll cut you out after all. You were anxious enough that she shouldn't marry me, I'll warrant, so what should she do but marry Robert instead, and do you out of the inheritance.' The chuckle became a laugh. 'Tell you what, Joseph, my boy, I'd even wish 'em well, just to see your mother's face when she hears the news.'

'I thank you, sir, for your kind wishes,' Joseph responded coldly. 'If I understand you correctly, however, the match is unlikely to be of long duration. It is to be hoped my brother can stand such notoriety as a divorce must bring.'

Claudius Lyle considered the young man dispassionately. 'I believe,' he said presently, 'that I have never liked you, Joseph. But now I find your company just too much to stomach. Good day to you!'

Joseph controlled himself with an effort. A strong retort was on his lips, which he would have regretted very much having spoken, so it was fortunate that the door opened at that moment to admit Wareing, who was looking harassed. 'What is it?' he demanded instead, glad to find someone unexceptional on whom to vent his spleen.

'My Lady Lyle, sir, is in the green saloon. She would seem, sir, to be in a state of some distress. She was wishful to see my master and appeared to be vastly put out when I was obliged to inform her he was away from Town.'

'Damnation!' Joseph exclaimed angrily. 'I suppose you told her I was here?'

'Yes, sir. She was inclined to meet you here, sir, until I informed her ladyship of Mr Lyle's presence, when she said she would await you in the saloon.'

Claudius gave a bark of laughter. 'Doesn't want to see me, eh? She knows I'll stand for none of her fainting fits! Go to her, Joseph, for the Lord's sake, and put the wretched woman out of her misery.'

Joseph scowled. There was much he wished to say to his great-uncle who deserved, in his opinion, a sharp set-down, but his legacy hung in the balance so with an effort he swallowed his hasty retort and executed a stiff bow. 'I will wish you a good day, sir,' he said coldly. 'It is to be hoped the next time we meet will be in happier circumstances.'

'At my funeral, if I've any say about it. No doubt that will be a happy day for you, Joseph. If,' he added with a malicious gleam in his eye, 'I don't decide to change m' will.'

Joseph Lyle said nothing. With a look of acute dislike on his face he gave his uncle another bow, and, accompanied by the old man's laughter, left the room.

He found his mother in a state of mild hysteria which

did little to calm his own harassed nerves. As he had supposed, someone had seen fit to inform her of her stepson's change of status, and it was to discover the truth that she had had herself conveyed to Berkeley Square. She lay, her smelling salts limply in her hand, upon her stepson's elegant gold sofa, and greeted her son, when he entered the room, with something approaching a wail.

'Joseph! Only tell me it can't be true! I declare I shall go distracted.'

Joseph, with as much patience as he could muster, retrieved the fallen bottle of salts and waved it irritably beneath her delicate nostrils. His mother opened her eyes.

'Joseph!' she wailed again, achieving an artistic shudder.

'Yes, Mama, it is I.'

'Oh, Joseph, such terrible news! Have you heard what they are saying about your brother? I won't believe it! I shan't permit it to be true.'

'Unfortunately, Mother, we have very little say in the matter. It would appear that my brother had indeed married the French female, but with any luck, mater dear, the marriage will be a short one.'

Lady Lyle had shuddered and closed her eyes again, but at the conclusion of her son's speech she opened them again and demanded what he meant by such a thing. 'For if you mean to tease me, Joseph, I tell you to your head that I'm in no mood for such humours. It is all a great deal too much for me to bear.'

'Do but have a little patience.' Joseph, his expression grim, had moved to a small mahogany table, and now poured brandy for them both from the decanter that stood there. 'I have no intention, you may be sure, of letting the marriage stand. I had thought to make my brother acquainted with the bride's true character, but since it would seem he is already familiar with it I shall have to think of something else. But don't worry. I have no intention of failing.'

Lady Lyle sipped suspiciously at the glass he had given her. 'Brandy, Joseph? Are you sure? Well, I suppose a very little.' She took a deep swallow and closed her eyes again. 'What did you mean when you spoke of the creature's true character? It is possible he has been deceived?'

'Unfortunately not, but he and I were the only ones not to be taken in. The creature's devilish cunning, I have to own it.'

'Really.' Lady Lyle was diverted enough to sit up. 'You mean she is not all she seems?'

Lyle gave a short laugh. 'Devil a bit! She's no more than a cursed adventuress. I guessed it almost from the first, but Robert, it would seem, was already informed. The lady, mater dear, is none other than the paragon our dearest uncle was to marry. Yes indeed! It would seem Robert followed her to London with the intention of bringing her to some sort of justice after she duped our uncle out of some of his precious blunt. We may surmise what occurred to make him change his mind.'

'Oh!' Lady Lyle exclaimed, 'it is even worse than I had thought! A common adventuress, in fact, no doubt without the slightest breeding. Oh!'

His mother had uttered a loud moan, and now fell back upon the sofa, her face alarmingly pale. Joseph, glancing at her in some disdain, was startled to see her looking truly ill and, gaining her in two long strides, demanded, 'Mother? What is amiss?'

'Joseph, the most appalling thought has just occurred

to me. Really, it is a great deal too bad of Robert.'

'Surely, Mama, that has not just occurred to you? Robert's behaviour has appeared dreadful to me for a great many years.'

His mother cast him a look of great reproach. 'Joseph, how can you be so unfeeling? That—hussy has taken my place! She will be mistress of Dearing, and, Joseph, it has just occurred to me, I shall be the Dowager Lady Lyle from now on. It is too much! She will have to go. You, Joseph, will have to do something.'

'I am relieved you agree with me, but at present just what course to take eludes me.'

'If only we could find out something about the wretched girl—that she was married already or some such thing. I suppose, Joseph, that such a thing is not possible?' Lady Lyle did not sound too hopeful.

Her son shook his head. 'Hardly, Mama, and since I do not know the creature's real name it is a little difficult to discover in any case.'

'Yes,' Lady Lyle said despondently, 'and no doubt it would be in some false name. Joseph, I believe I shall have a fit of the vapours.'

'Do so, Mama, with my good wishes, but I have work to do, so you will forgive me if I take my leave.'

His mother sat up. 'Do not leave me, Joseph, I beg of you. Why, that dreadful old man is here, and if I am obliged to be civil to him I believe it would kill me. Take me with you, Joseph, if you please.'

'I am driving a curricle, Mama, but I should be happy to deposit you in Half-Moon Street.'

'Well, I suppose if it must be your curricle it must, though I declare I shall never understand why you drive such a nasty, dangerous vehicle. I'm sure I expect every day to hear you have broke your neck.'

She was gathering hat and gloves as she spoke, and moved to pin her frivolous headwear into position before a long mirror. Her son watched her in silence for a moment or two and then smiled. 'I believe, Mama, that I never saw you in a more becoming hat. Do you know, if I find nothing is to be done about this wretched business I think I shall set about getting you a new husband. I dare say it should not be so very difficult, after all.'

His mother swung round, her face wreathed in smiles, her troubles forgotten. 'Do you really think so? It might be a good idea, I suppose.' She grimaced. 'Anything, after all, would be better than being known as The Dowager for the rest of my life.'

She laid her hand on her son's immaculate sleeve, and they left the room together.

CHAPTER
ELEVEN

THE fact that her new husband was half an hour late for dinner on their first evening together did not greatly disturb Genevieve. Wretched as she was, it was something of a relief to find the wide drawing-room quite empty, a log fire crackling busily within the hearth, and a general atmosphere of easiness and well-being abounding.

She seated herself in a large wing-chair, positioned at just the right distance from the fire, where she could appreciate its warmth without unpleasantly burning her face. It was only after she had sat there for nearly half an hour without disturbance of any kind that she began to wonder what had become of Sir Robert, and whether or not she should pull the bell-rope that dangled so closely at hand. Just as she was summoning her courage to do so the door opened to admit Sir Robert himself, dressed in a long tail-coat of olive superfine and pantaloons of the palest biscuit, so she tried to relax and greet her new husband with something approaching a smile. He held out his hand to her.

'Forgive me, I am so sorry to have kept you waiting. Did you ring for Grooby? There is some fine madeira, I am sure you would like it.'

'No, I did not like—'

'Did not like?' Sir Robert repeated, kissing her hand

with some gallantry before moving to pull the bell. 'You must not be nervous, you know. This is your home now. But perhaps madeira is not to your taste?'

He looked an inquiry, and she said quickly, 'Oh indeed, assuredly, I do not know what is amiss with me.'

'You are nervous, my love. Don't worry, I understand perfectly well.' He hesitated a moment and then, turning to the fire, said, 'You have no need to fear me, you know. I am not, perhaps, such a fool as you would think.' He turned, and smiled at her. 'There is plenty of time, my love, for us to get to know each other. You need not be afraid that I shall—importune you in any way.'

Genevieve blushed scarlet, and stammered something about being very obliged to him.

'I am aware of your reasons for marrying me, Valentine,' Sir Robert continued, 'but I am nothing if not patient.' He smiled, and carefully dusted a speck of snuff from his sleeve. 'I want nothing more than your happiness, I beg you to remember that.'

Genevieve would have answered, and indeed, had raised large, anxious eyes to his face when the door opened to admit the butler. Sir Robert ordered the madeira, and when the servant had departed the moment was lost, and Genevieve in control of herself again.

'You have your bills to hand, of course,' Sir Robert said easily, smiling kindly down at her. 'I wish you would let me have them.'

'M'sieur, that is very kind of you, *certainement*, but there is no need, *je vous assure*. If you would but give me—the money I shall travel to London tomorrow myself.'

Sir Robert frowned slightly. 'My dear, we have only

just left London! I assure you, there is not the slightest need for you to do such a thing. Only give me the bills and my man of business will settle them at once without any trouble to you at all.'

'That is very kind of you, m'sieur,' Genevieve said, smiling up at him with, she trusted, gratitude in her expression. ''Owever, I would greatly prefer to attend to the matter—personally. You 'ave been a great deal too kind already.'

Sir Robert shrugged. 'You must do as you wish, child. I am merely anxious that the unpleasant affair be settled as soon as possible that we may enjoy our honeymoon. You may, of course, have just as much money as you need.'

Genevieve said, '*Merci, m'sieur*,' in a voice so small as to be almost inaudible, and then fell to an examination of her hands until the butler returned.

During the dinner that followed Genevieve made some effort to appear cheerful, but it was an effort that cost her dearly. Sir Robert was so very solicitous for her comfort, anxious that she be neither too hot nor too cold, nor disturbed by the wicked draught that cut through the room, despite the thick aubusson, and the heavy curtains at all the windows. He attempted, too, to make light conversation on perfectly unexceptional topics, all of which served the more to make Genevieve feel she was treating him very badly indeed. More than once was she on the verge of telling him everything and taking her chance; it required self-control of the highest order to withold such inclinations and maintain her desperate charade. If only her husband had not been so very kind to her she would have found it all a great deal easier to bear! He spoke of any changes she might wish to make at Dearing, whether to the furnishings or the staff, saying she might do precisely as she chose. In fact, his only regret was that, since he was engaged to his bailiff the following day he could not accompany her to London to visit the necessary warehouses. Genevieve expressed what she hoped was suitable chagrin, but said that she was sure everything would be perfect, and besides, she could not think of making any changes until she had had a little time to look about her. Sir Robert merely nodded.

Genevieve retired to her bed feeling she had betrayed the whole world. Not only had she shown her beloved young brother such a poor example that he now stood in danger of ending his days on the gallows, or at the very least in some far-flung colony, but she intended to deceive even further a man from whom she had received nothing but kindness, and who was, besides, the embodiment of an ideal. In fact, she did not sleep at all, and when Mary entered the room the following morning with her chocolate she found her mistress already up and dressed, with the apparent intention of leaving as soon as was decently possible.

It was with some trepidation that she descended to the breakfast-room, knowing she must see Sir Robert before she left but dreading the meeting. In the event she need not have worried for a fat envelope reposed upon the table addressed 'To my wife', and containing a great deal more money than she had asked for. Genevieve's first reaction was one of intense relief, but when her casually posed question produced from the servant the response that the master had already ridden out with Jarvis, the bailiff, she knew only a sense of despair, and irretrievable loss. It was unlikely, she knew, that they would ever meet again.

In an attempt to banish such depressing thoughts

Genevieve turned her attention reluctantly to the day ahead of her, forcing herself to make some kind of plan. Her husband had arranged for a carriage to take her back to London—she would need to dispose of it somehow without exciting the coachman's suspicions until it was too late for anything to be done. The thought that the poor fellow might be considerably alarmed by her sudden disappearance occurred to her as he handed her into the luxurious interior of the coach, and she could only hope that his master would not blame this unfortunate worthy for his wife's departure.

The journey was accomplished in an amazingly short space of time, it seemed to Genevieve, lost as she was in some abstraction. Mary, at her side, was likewise thoughtful, and the two covered the short distance with hardly a word being exchanged. She had no desire for the coachman to know precisely where her business was to be conducted, so she asked to be set down outside Jones's, in Bond Street, saying she would walk on to the library, where he might collect her in one hour. Accordingly the carriage drew up outside the haberdashers, they were set down, and the coachman whipped up his horses again, leaving Genevieve to stare disconsolately after him.

'Mary, how I wish it did not have to be so!' she exclaimed impulsively, turning to hail a passing hackney. 'Will he ever forgive me?'

'Since you are unlikely ever to see him again I'm sure it cannot signify if he does not,' Mary remarked dryly, climbing after her mistress into the cab.

'How despicable it all is,' Genevieve continued, giving no appearance of having heard her maid speak. 'I'm sure if I had had the least notion of how it would be I should never have embarked on the whole horrid business. Oh,

Mary,' she turned impulsively to her maid, 'whatever will become of me now?'

'Lor', Miss Gen, you should have thought of that before, it seems to me. Maggots in your brain, that's what you've got.'

Genevieve sighed. 'I begin to think you're right, Mary,' she said despondently. 'It's all for George's sake, after all. It is most selfish of me to be thinking of myself when he is in such trouble.'

Mary shook her head, but refrained from comment.

The hole in which George was ensconced looked more dismal than ever, Genevieve thought, having lost her heart to a rambling mansion in Kent. She heard Mary draw breath beside her as she pushed open the worm-eaten door and exposed the rickety stairs leading to the landing, but she firmly put to one side those thoughts that would keep intruding, so unwelcomely, upon her resolve. As they approached the stairs they heard a door open above them, and in a moment a young woman with hair of a startling yellow leaned over the banisters to peer at them.

'Ho, so it's you, is it?' she remarked, recognising Genevieve. 'Thought you weren't coming. Taken your time, 'aven't you? Who's the mort with you?'

'This is Mary, my maid. This, Mary, is the kind soul who has taken care of poor George in his trouble. I am greatly indebted to her.'

Mary, gaining the landing behind her mistress, surveyed the kind soul with suspicion and received in her turn a cackle of laughter.

'Lord luv us, she's a peery mort and no mistake! Maid, is she? Well, you'd better come with me, but 'ave a care! Dicked in the nob, 'e is. On the mop. Gin,' she added, seeing the non-comprehension.

'Dear God,' Genevieve murmured, following the young woman into the room.

Her brother still lay upon the truckle-bed, but it was plain from the first that all was not well. He had lost weight since Genevieve had last seen him, and his eyes now stared at her from huge, sunken sockets. There were purple rings about them, and his face had a greyish tinge she could not like.

'Hello, dearest,' she said, coming and sitting on the end of the bed. 'Are you feeling any better? I have the money.'

The young man, who had struggled into a sitting position when she entered the room, collapsed against the pillows and whispered, 'Thank God.' He closed his eyes, and Genevieve, in some alarm, looked at Nell, but the young woman merely shrugged, and jerked her head towards the grimy window.

A man stood there, a man whom Genevieve had not previously noticed, which said much for her preoccupation, since the gentleman occupied the entire window embrasure, almost completely obliterating the light. Mr Smith was really rather a large gentleman, with a large, balding pate he wiped continuously with a grubby kerchief.

'If you have the money,' he said, moving forward with small, agitated steps, 'we must be on our way. I have waited too long as it is and we must reach Dover before dawn.'

Once more the man on the bed struggled to sit up. 'You'll remember what I said? You'll take my sister too?'

The man sighed and mopped his brow again. 'If that's what you want. But I warn you, it won't be easy.'

George grimaced. 'Damn you, do you think I could travel on my own?'

'No, I don't suppose you could,' Mr Smith said, after surveying George briefly out of small, piggy eyes. 'But not the maid.'

'Not Mary?' Genevieve exclaimed. 'But she must come.'

'You may please yourself, miss,' Mr Smith said, 'but if you take the maid you'll not travel with me. I cannot be responsible for so many persons.'

'Never you mind, Miss Gen,' Mary said soothingly as Genevieve made to argue the point. 'I can follow easy enough in a day or two with Mr Collins. There's nothing I know of to stop us leaving the country like honest citizens.'

Genevieve hesitated. 'No, Mary, you are quite right. Forgive me, I was not thinking. I dare say it will be a great deal more comfortable for you in any event. But you will need money.' Opening the envelope Sir Robert had given her she counted out a number of bills, thought for a moment, and then added one more. 'We shall meet in Paris, Mary, in the house in the Rue St Dominique. Do not fail me!'

'As if I should even consider such a thing!' Mary exclaimed indignantly. 'Me and Collins, I dare say we shouldn't know what to do without you and Mr George, so don't you worrit yourself about us. We'll be as right as a trivet.'

The young woman paused, and then nodded. 'Of course. Thank you, Mary, for everything.' With a forced smile she leaned forward and kissed the maid on her cheek. 'Now go, before I make a fool of myself.'

'Now then, Miss Gen, none of that, if you please. And you, Master George, don't you let your mistress get into mischief, for you know as well as I what she's like. Are you listening, Master George?'

George, from his truckle-bed, smiled feebly and intimated that he was.

'Good. Then I'll be off.' Her gaze swept past the nervous Mr Smith to rest briefly upon the kind soul, then she sniffed, and in a moment had left the room.

Mary gained the street in a minute. The hackney in which she and Genevieve had come still stood in the street but she ignored it, turning and walking purposefully in the direction of St Paul's. She had gone barely a hundred yards before she heard the sound of hooves and, turning, saw a darkly shadowed figure upon a roan mare bearing down upon her. She stopped, and in a moment he had drawn level.

'They travel immediately,' she said briskly, glancing back towards the house she had left. 'They must reach Dover before dawn.' She saw the man above her nod his head shortly, and she added, 'Please to have a care, sir! I have such a feeling, I cannot explain it.'

For a moment the figure did not answer and then he said shortly, 'Have no fear, Mary, I am not unarmed. No harm shall befall your mistress, of that you may be sure.'

'Thank you, sir, but what of my young master? He's in a parlous sad taking, and no mistake.'

'Can he walk?'

Mary shook her head. 'Undoubtedly not, sir! But I must be going. It would never do for them to see me talking to you here.'

The figure nodded. 'Make for Dearing, Mary, without delay, and you had better find that wretched boy's servant. Chances are we'll have need of him there.' He thought for a moment and then said, 'Ask my butler to send for the doctor. I have no doubt but that he will be required.'

Mary did not answer. Down the road, she saw a figure

appear in the doorway of the house she had just left, so without further ado she walked away, leaving the solitary horseman to go about his business.

Sir Robert had spent the night in earnest contemplation of the situation. What Mary had told him had thrown abundant light upon his awkward love's actions, and he had desired more than anything that evening to take her in his arms and tell her not to be such a little fool. That he had not done so was greatly to his credit, but he had, as a result, spent the night restlessly tossing upon his couch, ideas forming and reforming in his brain only to be mulled over and discarded. By morning he had reached no firm resolve of what his actions should be; he only knew that he had no intention of letting his newly acquired bride slip so easily away. Consequently, when he had supposedly been deep in conversation with his bailiff he was, in fact, already mounted upon his roan, and watching his wife's departure from a small rise in his own park.

He had followed her up to London. It was no easy feat to pass unnoticed through the famous streets but he had done so, and now, as he watched over his shoulder, he was wondering just how long his luck would hold. A fat man had come into the street and now approached the hackney that yet waited. A few words were exchanged, and then a moment later Sir Robert saw three more figures emerge, the middle one supported by the other two. The central figure seemed to be more carried than walking; if this were George he was in a bad case indeed. Together the two women managed to hoist their burden into the carriage. There was a discussion between them and something changed hands. Then one, his wife, Sir Robert knew, climbed into the carriage, and in a moment the door had been shut and the carriage moved away. For a moment or two Sir Robert waited, and then he turned his horse, and trotted up the street after them.

Like his brother Joseph Lyle had spent much of the evening in thought. He had dined alone, for which he was grateful, since his mother could only have been a disturbing influence, fond though he was of her. But the Dowager Lady Lyle, as she must now be known, had banished cares sufficiently to be able to accept an invitation to dine with an old friend, a retired Major, in fact, and his sister at Grillon's Hotel. So Joseph was alone; alone he sat over his port, lingering far longer than his cherished parent might have thought polite, turning over the events of the morning. Try as he would there was no way that he could see out of the problem. Since his brother knew as much as he, nay, probably more, there was little to be gained by impetuous revelation. Of course, he could hire some fellow to delve into her past—there were people who did such things, he knew— but it would be an added expense when he was running perilously short of funds, and besides, he had a curious suspicion that Mlle Deneuve, the new Lady Lyle, would be expert in covering her tracks. Lyle smiled sourly into his glass. He had to admit it, the wench was extremely clever, cleverer even than himself, he suspected, although it cost him a pang to own it. At any other time he might have appreciated the tangling with such a female—it might have its own rewards, after all, and Mlle Deneuve was far from unattractive—but just at the moment, when his affairs were in such a shaky state he could not afford the effort. Why, only that morning he had received a highly unpleasant missive from his tailor, intimating that the instant settling of his account would be highly appreciated, and he knew that it could only be a matter of time before he received similar notes from his other creditors. No, an entanglement with Mlle Deneuve was not to be contemplated, but she did have to be removed, and that quickly. Holding up his glass Lyle examined the contents abstractedly. There must be some way, he knew, of achieving it, and without leaving the trail of his passing.

He awoke with no more idea than when he had finally fallen asleep. Since this had occurred well into the following morning it was past noon before he finally quitted his chamber, and sauntered downstairs to partake of a leisurely luncheon. As he swallowed hot coffee and stared absently through the long window he made a sudden decision, and rose from the table without more ado. In a moment his curricle had been summoned; in less than half an hour he was seated in it, heading at a smart pace for Dearing. It was the action of impulse—he knew not what could possibly be gained by the journey, and yet something told him that the game could yet be his, if only he played it aright. The day was dull and grey, not the day for a casual drive, and his groom sat hunched beside him, his coat collar upturned, as they sped through the London streets. It had not been early when they started, consequently their pace was fast; Joseph had no desire to be caught by failing daylight: it was the season of the highway robber.

For some little while his optimism carried him along. Since the day was indeed so inauspicious he met none of the casual traffic so loathed by the determined traveller—the lumbering landaus and smart barouches. Instead his only obstacle on the first stage proved to be a mail-coach, and he contrived to pass this with ease. At the first change it was necessary to delay to arrange the return of his own horses but, this being done, and the new team poled up, he was on his way again his optimism

very little abated. He continued in this happy state as far
as Blackheath, where he came up behind a heavy accom-
modation coach that hugged the middle of the road. He
was obliged to proceed behind it for some miles before
the road became wide enough for him to pass with ease.
And then, too, he caused his groom to clutch frantically
at the side of the carriage for in his anxiety to pass the
wretched vehicle he quite failed to notice a smart tilbury
being driven at some speed in the opposite direction.
Seeing it at the last minute Joseph pulled sharply on his
reins, swinging the curricle neatly in front of the accom-
modation coach and passing the tilbury with an inch or
two to spare. Joseph glanced at his groom's grim countenance and grinned.

The day continued dry though grey until Shooter's
Hill was reached, but as the team dropped back to a
steady trot to take the hill a sharp gust of wind blew a fine
mizzle at them. This proved to be but the herald of
something stronger and altogether wilder, and very soon
Joseph was hunching his shoulders against driving rain.
Beside him his groom sat silent and miserable; this was
by no means his idea of a pleasant day out. His master,
besides, was driving his animals harder than he would
have cared for, bowling along at a pace that made the
rain sting his eyes and soak him through to the skin.
They reached the top of Shooter's Hill and began a rapid
descent, his master now holding the animals firmly in
check. Then level ground was gained once more and
Lyle's breakneck speed resumed.

There were now a mere eight miles to cover, and for a
moment Joseph considered them without making a further change. The beasts had been driven hard however,
and indeed, just as he was deliberating within himself
one of his wheelers went lame and the pace was reduced

to a walk. Bexley approached, and Joseph told the groom to blow up for a change. This he did, and as they entered the yard of the inn ostlers were already running out to attend to him. Another vehicle stood in the yard, a hired chaise, and ostlers were leading away four steaming horses. Disinterestedly Joseph allowed his gaze to wander over the equipage, and found that gaze caught. Abruptly he turned his head away. For a moment he pondered, and then, as the ostlers began to pole up the new team he said shortly, 'I've changed my mind. I shall leave my curricle here for tonight. Have you a horse for hire? I intend to continue my journey on horseback.'

The fellow to whom this was addressed hesitated for a moment clearly deeming a person who would take to horseback in a storm as being of unsound mind. It being far from his place to quibble, however, he merely nodded and signified that if the gentleman would care to step down an animal would be made ready immediately. It was left to Joseph's groom to stare, which he did, and then asked if he was required to proceed on horseback also.

'What? Oh no, Henry, thank you. Get yourself a room. If I don't return by morning you had better do something about getting my curricle back to London. I shall have made other arrangements.'

'Very good, sir.' Henry said no more. If his master had chosen today to take leave of his senses if was not up to him to object. As long as he continued to pay him it was no concern of his.

An animal by this time had been saddled and made ready, and was now led into the yard, its head drooping miserably. Joseph cast an impatient eye over the brute, sighed, and signalled his approval. The rain was now driving hard at them as they stood in the cobbled yard, but Lyle did not appear to notice as he swung himself into the high saddle. Henry, glad at least that his work was over for the day shrugged, and, turning, did not wait to see his master ride from the yard.

The other carriage had, by this time, received its new team, and was once more on its way. As Joseph trotted away from the inn he saw it swaying along the rutted road ahead of him. Accordingly he turned up his coat, hunched his shoulders, and set his wretched mount at a smart trot. He could hardly believe his good fortune. The casual glance he had cast at the waiting carriage had been no more than a cursory inspection; it was with considerable surprise that he had recognised one of its occupants as being the young woman lately known to him as Mlle Deneuve. Who were the others was of no concern to him once he realised his brother was not with them. He saw clearly how it must have been. Mlle Deneuve, for some reason, had spent the night in the Metropolis, and was now travelling to Dearing where, he presumed, his brother would be found. And now, at last, a plan—daring, it was true—began to suggest itself to Mr Lyle. The daylight was failing rapidly, considerably aided by the darkened sky: in half an hour it would be dark. Dearing was not an hour away, but there was yet time for him to put his scheme into effect. The carriage ahead of him was travelling as fast as might reasonably have been thought safe upon a road that was threatening to turn into a running stream; he would need to think very quickly indeed. Lyle did not consider such a thing to be beyond him. They were approaching an area of open land that was reasonably familiar to him since he had been wont to play there as a boy. It was unfortunate that Watling Street ran particularly straight just now, but Lyle was satisfied that the weather, together with the darkened sky, would mean very little risk. At the thought of it he experienced a thrill in the pit of his stomach and he patted the pocket of his greatcoat. His pistols, elaborate weapons with pearl handles, lay there snugly, the addition of an impulse, and, it transpired, his probable salvation. He could see it now so plainly, could hear the screams of the women, the startled and frightened expressions of the men, too cowardly to do more than gape at the weapon he held. It was all too perfect for words. At the thought of such a neat end to the affair he could barely control his impatience. His heart thumped unpleasantly in his chest, his throat grew dry, and his palms became warm and damp. But his thinking remained crystal-clear; in fact, he rather thought his brain was working a great deal better than usual. In a matter of minutes the whole beautiful plan lay before him. It would be necessary to square Henry, of course, but he could return for his curricle in a very short space of time, even be back in London for a late dinner. The more he thought about it the more pleased he became, and the more anxious to be done with delay. But now the country opened out before him. Ahead the carriage was labouring through a particularly muddy stretch of road; a glance over his shoulder assured him that no other vehicle was in sight. With fingers that trembled Joseph drew one of the pistols from his pocket and cocked it gently. At the pressure of his heels his patient mount lengthened its stride, and he veered from the road slightly to give the carriage a wider berth. Within a couple of minutes he had passed it and wheeled around: the carriage now swung and clattered its way towards him. He could see clearly the two hunched figures on the box and wondered briefly if they had noticed him yet and, if so, whether they would be armed. But it was all one. Coachmen and grooms were notoriously cowardly, besides being obliged to use that appallingly cumbersome weapon, the blunderbuss. At the last minute he dragged a kerchief from his pocket and succeeded, with some fumbling, in tying it about the lower part of his face. At his urging the mare stepped obediently into the centre of the road and stood there, head drooping slightly, while her rider raised his arm and took careful aim.

Within the coach all was silent, save for the groaning and creaking of springs and the rattling of the carriage's ancient joints. Genevieve sat dully in one corner staring with unseeing eyes through the greasy window, seeing all the time that rather grim countenance with its determined jaw and the smile that could still do unpredictable things to a maiden's heart. George was slumped at her side dozing lightly with his head resting on her shoulder. His fevered utterances had occupied Genevieve for quite a few miles, but it was some time now since he had dropped into an uneasy slumber. The other occupant was very wide awake, and sat erect against the squabs, his fat fingers twisting nervously in his lap. He had the most peculiar sensation that something was going to go sadly awry, although he could not think what this could possibly be since his plans had been laid with great exactness. Many times had he made this particular journey, escorting penniless young gentlemen out of reach of their creditors and wild young gentlemen with a passion for duelling out of the reach of the law. He knew perfectly well that nothing could go wrong, but ever since they had made that last change he had had the strangest sensation of foreboding. It was all nonsense, of course. He was a fool. With this comforting thought the gentleman eased himself slightly in his seat and composed himself for slumber.

The occupants of the carriage did not hear the shot for the noise of their progress deadened all else, but they felt its consequence. There came a shout from the box above them, accompanied by the snorting of terrified animals. The carriage seemed to be swaying rather more than was normal, sufficiently, in fact, to jerk George from his slumber and cast him against the unfortunate Mr Smith. Genevieve, rudely aroused from her reverie, leaned forward to let down the window and peer into the gloom ahead. For a moment just what had occurred remained obscure. To be sure, the coachman was dragging on the reins in a manner usually forbidden, and the horses were responding in a fashion that was far from normal, bucking and rearing within the traces, one doing his best to bolt and drag his fellows with him. Genevieve frowned and started to address the man above her when a figure in the road caught her attention and she drew in her head rather quickly.

'Mr Smith,' she said breathlessly, turning large eyes towards that perplexed gentleman, 'have you a pistol about you? If so, I beseech you to have it ready. We are waylaid.'

'Highwaymen!' This from George, who had struggled once more into an upright position. Genevieve glanced at him. His eyes were unnaturally bright and his face was in high flush. 'I have always wanted to be held up,' the young man continued dreamily, 'and it has to happen when I am laid by the heels.'

He spoke in a voice of pique, and Genevieve controlled her exasperation with an effort. 'I wonder if this weapon is loaded,' she said, drawing a cumbersome pistol from the holster at her side. 'Unfortunately there is little time to find out.'

'My dear Miss Christy!' exclaimed Mr Smith, eyeing her efforts to cock the weapon with alarm. 'I beg of you, return that object to its holster! I have a pistol, and besides, you may shoot yourself before ever injuring the ruffians who are waylaying us. Do sit still, I beg of you!'

'Really, Mr Smith, how paltry. Do you suppose you will be able to hold them off on your own? What is this little nob for here? Ah, I have it.' She leaned out of the window as she spoke, levelled the weapon as best she could and resolutely pulled the trigger. There was a disappointing click. Mr Smith breathed again. 'It was not loaded,' she announced, pulling her head inside. 'Indeed, Mr Smith, I hope you are a reasonable shot for our dependence is now upon you.'

Mr Smith eyed her resentfully, and seemed about to argue the point when the carriage finally rolled to a halt.

'Highwaymen!' George muttered again, sliding down against Genevieve's shoulder and closing his eyes.

'George, please!' that afflicted damsel cried. 'Do but sit up, I beg of you!'

'It's all right,' Mr Smith said, peering out of the window, 'there is only one, as far as I can see. He should be very little trouble at all.'

'I hope you may be right,' Genevieve answered earnestly, trying ineffectually to return her brother to an upright position.

Outside, Joseph had levelled his pistol threateningly at the coachman, who had already persuaded the groom to toss aside the awkward blunderbuss. The groom, who had been perfectly willing to discharge the cumbersome weapon in the direction of the highwayman's brain, thought this very paltry behaviour indeed and did not scruple to say so.

'Be quiet,' the coachman growled at him. 'You might get paid to die, but I certainly don't. He's got no business with us, so just hold your peace.'

'Wise words,' Joseph remarked, grinning behind his handkerchief. 'Perhaps you would be good enough to step down from your box, then we may be certain of your good will.'

'I hope you know what you're about, that's all,' the groom grumbled as he jumped into the muddy road. 'I heard tell of a highwayman who stole a coach in just such circumstances as these, so I hope you intend to do the explaining.'

The coachman scowled, and dropped into the road at the side of the groom. 'You just hold your peace, young Bill,' he said grimly, keeping one eye upon the masked figure, 'or I'll have young Tom up with me next time out.'

Having satisfied himself that the groom and coachman intended no mischief Joseph urged his mare up to the side of the carriage. Leaning down, he wrenched open the door, dragging the unfortunate Mr Smith into the mud as he did so.

'Now then, who is this?' Joseph wondered aloud, eyeing the fallen figure with amusement in his eyes. 'It would seem to me that he is armed. Does he intend me some harm, perhaps? Should I shoot him now, or later?'

Beneath him in the mud the unhappy Mr Smith rolled over onto his back and goggled at the huge figure above him. 'No, no, don't shoot, I beg of you! You may have all my money, and my watch as well. Here!' He scrambled to his feet as he spoke, fumbling in his pocket for his purse, which, after a moment, he held out in his grubbied hand. 'Take it! And my watch too if you like! Here!'

Joseph laughed. 'A paltry purse, sir? Come now, do you take me for a flat? The rolls of soft, if you please.'

'Rolls of soft? But this is all I have.'

Joseph's eyes leered wickedly at him over the handkerchief. 'Indeed? Perhaps you would remember better if I shot you a little? In the stomach, say?'

Mr Smith trembled. There was something strangely deadly about this peculiarly well-spoken highwayman, something he could very much wish he had not detected. 'Oh, very well,' he muttered, searching once more in his pockets. 'Here, take it! I'm sure I do not care.'

'That is very kind of you, my good fellow,' Joseph replied silkily, receiving the roll of bills from the reluctant Mr Smith. 'Perhaps you would be good enough to hand me that little pistol you discarded when you fell. By the muzzle, if you please. I should not care to have it discharge accidentally.'

Mr Smith hesitated for a moment. He had, foolishly, he now realised, supposed his pistol to have been forgotten. To have to surrender it to this ruffian was really a great deal too bad. Nevertheless, he stooped to retrieve it, panting a little, and handed it to the masked scoundrel above him, his only hope that it might have become blocked by the mud in which it had lain.

Joseph smiled. 'Thank you, my friend,' he said, pocketing the weapon with due care. Urging his mare forward he came abreast of the carriage once more and peered through the open door. 'Dear me!' he exclaimed, feigning surprise. 'Fair Diana, and injured swain? Or is he merely ailing? Well, it doesn't signify one way or the other. Be good enough to descend, Diana, that I might view you the better.'

For a moment Genevieve contemplated the masked man in silence. Then, 'My brother is injured. He cannot walk and would be quite unable to descend from the carriage as you ask.'

The highwayman raised his brows. 'Injured indeed! If that is truly the case he can be of little danger to me, but I think I shall look at him nevertheless.' He urged his mare closer still, to see the better into the dim interior. 'Your brother, Diana? He looks uncommon ill, to be sure!'

At the sound of the voice George opened his eyes again, and, after struggling to focus them, pronounced thickly, 'You're that cursed highwayman! Should have shot you. Haven't got a pistol. Forgot it.' So saying he slumped against Genevieve's shoulder again and shut his eyes.

'Please,' Genevieve said imploringly, 'surely you can see he is delirious!'

The highwayman frowned for a moment and then said curtly, 'Very well, but you may descend. I wish for a better look at you.'

Genevieve raised her chin a little. 'Sir, I have no intention of descending from the carriage. There can be no possible need for it, unless you intend to abduct me, or some such thing, and that would be utterly pointless.'

The highwayman's eyes glinted. 'I do not intend such a thing, but who is to say you are not armed? Why, if I let you be, perhaps you may shoot me with some concealed weapon.'

'I have no weapon,' Genevieve assured him angrily, 'or I would have shot you all ready. In fact I tried to do so but the pistols in this carriage are not loaded.'

Joseph smiled into his handkerchief. 'In that case, ma'am, I think you had better descend this instant. I should hate to be compelled to shoot you for your recalcitrance. It would be such a terrible waste.'

Genevieve hesitated. There was something, she decided, strangely familiar about the man before her, something about his voice that she recognised. She felt that if she had only had time she would have discovered him somewhere amongst her acquaintance. She said musingly, 'Don't I know you? Haven't we met somewhere before?'

The eyes glinted at her again. 'Quite possible, Diana. Perhaps I have held you up before.'

Miss Christy shook her head. 'No, I don't think so,' she said firmly.

'You are wasting time, Diana. Are you going to get our, or do I have to come in and fetch you?'

For a moment Genevieve considered him and then she smiled slightly. 'Yes, sir, you do.'

'Very well,' the highwayman exclaimed, kicking his feet free of the stirrups, 'I shall!'

Growing alarmed now Genevieve watched as the man sprang from his horse, obviously with the intention of approaching her. In spite of her bold words she felt frightened by his manner, and shrank a little against her slumbering brother. 'George,' she whispered urgently, 'do wake up!'

But George, far away, did not hear her.

The highwayman was now filling the doorway, and although Genevieve could no longer see his face she could hear him laugh softly as he set one foot inside. Then a curious sound broke from his mouth and he seemed to reel strangely, almost drunkenly. He recovered in an instant and, turning back through the door, fired a single shot. There was the sound of a falling weight, and then the highwayman turned back to her.

'Whatever have you done?' Genevieve cried, starting up. 'Who have you shot? Not Mr Smith?'

'The very same, if that is your cumbersome friend. I regret that it is a flesh wound merely. No doubt he will recover soon enough.'

'How could you!' Genevieve demanded, her eyes flaming. 'I'm sure I never knew such a coward to shoot an unarmed man!'

The highwayman chuckled. 'So unarmed he could hit me over the head with a stick. But never mind.' Reaching in, he caught Genevieve by the arm and dragged her forward.

She struggled violently, calling upon her brother to assist her, but he did not wake, having substituted the side of the carriage for his sister's shoulder. She was out of the carriage and standing in mud, and there before her was the slumped form of Mr Smith, bleeding profusely from a wound in his arm. 'Poor Mr Smith! You must let me help him.'

'I've told you, he'll be well enough. I shouldn't like to have to shoot him again because you had been foolish enough to rouse him.'

Genevieve fell silent. Standing at a little distance were the coachman and groom, but she could not feel that they would be of the least use to her.

'Now, Diana,' the highwayman said, swinging her to face him, 'let me see you.'

She looked mutinously up at him, and he laughed. 'So brave, so young, fair sweet! Do you know, I've a mind to abduct you after all.'

He dragged her closer, and Genevieve steeled herself for his embrace when there came a sharp report and the sound of an approaching horse. Someone shouted, and the highwayman cursed. Before she knew what he would be at he had swung her onto his horse, mounted behind, and, pulling sharply upon the reins, was leaving the scene at a gallop. Genevieve screamed, but even to her ears it was a paltry sound, and she cursed herself for being fool enough to have put the idea into the fellow's head. Now they were being pursued, doubtless by some foolhardy fellow bent upon his own glory, who would have no scruple about firing at them as they fled. But this was a pointless fear. Her main danger, at that moment, seemed to be of falling from a galloping horse, something which, even in these circumstances, she had no desire to do. The mare, startled by the shot and her rider's obvious urgency, had taken to a headlong flight, and now proceeded across the heath in a manner so wild that Genevieve wondered at her captor's ability to check it. And now, too, trees were looming ahead; they would need to drop at least to a trot if they were not all to come to disaster. She tried to turn her head to see their pursuer, but the highwayman's grip upon her tightened painfully. She could hear nothing above the pounding of their own animal's hooves and the beat of her heart, which was so loud as to make thinking an impossibility. The trees were almost before them; she shut her eyes, and waited for the inevitable accident. It did not come. After what seemed an interminable time the motion of the horse beneath her was noticeably slackened; they no longer proceeded in a straight line; indeed, they seemed rather to be weaving a path around something. Genevieve opened her eyes again. They were in dense woodland, the trees growing so closely together that in the failing daylight it was impossible to see very far. The mare beneath her was proceeding at a walk, and seemed grateful for the respite, for the sweat streamed from her neck and her breath came in short bursts. Genevieve guessed she was nearly spent.

'I hope you know,' she said, glancing up at the masked

face, 'that you can be hanged for what you have done.'

The highwayman did not answer. His attention seemed to be all on the ground before him, and then Genevieve realised that he was listening intently.

'Let me go,' Genevieve whispered urgently. 'I shall say nothing, I promise you.'

'I'm afraid, Lady Lyle,' the highwayman said, 'that I can never let you go. I have perjured myself.'

'You know who I am!' Genevieve exclaimed. 'Then you know that my husband is a very wealthy man. I am sure he would be willing to pay handsomely for my return.'

He glanced briefly at her. 'Do you know, that is something that had never occurred to me? I had thought to kill you, but perhaps—' He paused, seemingly deep in meditation.

'Kill me?' Genevieve gasped. 'Whatever for? Why, I don't even know you.'

'Do you not? You would have been wise, Lady Lyle, to have accepted defeat—I do not offer idle threats. When you married my brother you signed your death warrant.'

'Your brother?' Genevieve stared. 'Then I do know you. Mr Lyle, why are you doing this? It is all foolishness. Had you but left well alone I should have been out of the country by tonight. It's true I married your brother, but he may have it annulled. Do, please, let me go!'

'I can't,' Joseph said shortly. 'Don't you know who our pursuer is? Didn't you recognise your own husband?'

'Robert? But it couldn't be he.'

'I assure you, it is. So you see, there is not the least

particle of use in my letting you go. You are my sole hope.'

Genevieve thought rapidly. 'No, wait. He can't possibly know who you are. He probably thinks you're a true highwayman. Why should he think otherwise? Oh do, please, let me go! I shan't tell him anything, I promise. You may be back in London before he even knows you've left.'

Slowly Joseph pulled away the handkerchief. 'How do I know I can trust you?' he said, smiling wryly at her. 'You are, by your own admission, nothing but an adventuress, a fortune seeker. Why should I believe anything you say? I'm sure, if I were in your position, I should say precisely the same thing, without meaning one word. Why should you leave now, just when you have everything you want?'

'There are reasons,' Genevieve said shortly, 'but I do not intend to discuss them with you.'

'Of course not. They do not exist. No, Mlle Deneuve—Lady Lyle—I think I shall retain what I have.'

'You are making a very grave mistake,' Genevieve began when Joseph held up his hand.

'Do you hear a horse?'

Genevieve paused, and listened. After a moment she said, 'I hear nothing, but the wind.'

'I'm sure I heard something,' Joseph persisted. 'Be quiet a minute.'

Genevieve obliged, but could hear nothing.

'He's here somewhere,' Joseph said, urging his horse into a walk. 'I don't trust him. I wonder why he was following you?'

Genevieve was wondering that, too. She could only suppose he had come upon the chaise by accident and had given chase without realising who had been taken captive. There was no reason that she could see for him to have been following the chaise at all, as Joseph seemed to think he had been. She would not have chosen to see him again, just when she had reconciled herself to the necessity of living without him, but if he were her only hope then there could be no help for it. How she would subsequently explain her presence in a hired chaise with two strange men she would consider later. At the moment she concerned herself with straining her ears as hard as her captor.

Joseph had urged his horse onward. His conviction that his brother was surreptitiously following led him to place one hand across Genevieve's mouth, at which she uttered a squeak in protestation.

'If you love your life keep quiet!' Joseph growled in her ear. 'I have nothing to lose, I assure you, and should not hesitate to cut your throat.'

Genevieve was silent. The hand pressed unpleasantly across her mouth and against her nose, restricting her breathing and pulling her head back painfully against his chest. Every nerve taut she strained her ears for any sound of Robert's horse, but there was none. She could only assume Joseph had been mistaken. She began to see that there would be no escape, that she would end her days here in this barren wood, and he buried under rotting leaves. Strangely she found no terror in this prospect. If Robert could not rescue her it seemed quite reasonable that she should perish. She could not even bring herself to worry about George, since Mary would certainly take care of him once he had arrived in France. There was the journey, of course, but he would survive that. He had, she decided, a much greater capacity for survival than herself, and wondered that she had never noticed it before when she had been so concerned about

his welfare. It would be George, and not she, who came
out of this present difficulty with a whole skin; George,
who had had not the slightest notion of how to conduct
himself, who had had no precise plan at all, who would
arrive safely in France whilst she, whose plan had been
determined down to the last detail, would fail at the last,
undone by a brother's greed.

While these thoughts flashed through her brain
Joseph had urged his horse onwards, and now, ahead of
them, came an increase in light that signified the end of
the wood. Genevieve became sensible of it when a sigh
escaped her captor and she felt the animal beneath her
lengthen its stride again. They were nearly out of the
wood, and she had not been rescued. It was just as she
had resigned herself to the inevitable that there was a
loud report and something whistled by unpleasantly
close to her ear. Above her Joseph cursed, and the
animal wheeled about. With one hand across Genevieve's mouth he was considerably handicapped, and
now struggled to free his pistol from the folds of his
greatcoat, in which it had become entangled.

'Stop precisely where you are,' came a cooly crisp
voice from somewhere behind them, 'I have you
covered, and should not hesitate to put the second
bullet through your brain.'

Genevieve heard her captor draw his breath in sharply, and then felt the cold muzzle of his pistol as he
pressed it against her temple.

Gently removing his hand from her mouth Joseph
hissed, 'Tell him not to shoot. Even if he kills me my
reflexes will pull the trigger. You will die in any event.'

For a moment Genevieve was silent, then as Joseph
said again, 'Tell him!' she opened her mouth and tried to
call out.

The sound was pathetic and unintelligible. She tried again. 'Robert?'

'Valentine! Are you all right?'

She nodded, and then, 'Yes. But he threatens to kill me if you shoot at him. He will, I am sure.'

'You would be advised to listen to the little lady, brother,' Joseph advised him dryly. 'I have, after all, little to lose.'

There was a moment's silence. 'Don't be a fool, Joseph,' Sir Robert said then from his place of conceal-ment. 'I have no intention of letting you get away with this particular folly, however lax I may have been in the past. Release my wife, and we shall discuss what is to be done.'

'No, I thank you. I've had enough of your generosity, Robert, I'll have none of your allowances.'

'I'm not talking of allowances. Release my wife and I'll make you a present of, say, thirty thousand pounds? That should be enough to satisfy even you for a while.'

For a moment Joseph was silent, and Genevieve thought he was really considering the offer. Then he laughed. 'I'm sorry, Robert, but it's not good enough. I'm sure Lady Lyle will be most disappointed to learn how little you value her.'

There was no answer for more than a minute, but then Sir Robert said, 'Very well, what do you want?'

'Dearing, by deed of gift, plus all the money you have in the Funds.' He laughed. 'You think I'm over-ambitious, perhaps, but I should tell you, Robert, that I had every intention of disposing of you as well, so really you are escaping very lightly. Oh, and since I do not value your word I should tell you that Lady Lyle will not be released to you until the deed of gift is in my posses-sion, so you had better let us pass.'

Genevieve sat thinking furiously. The whole thing, she decided, was utterly monstrous, and she had no intention of letting Robert be so badly used, and for someone as worthless as herself. That Joseph intended to kill her in any event she no longer doubted; his refusal to release her confirmed this fact. Since she was destined to die, therefore, it seemed only reasonable that she should save Robert such a ridiculous expense on her account. Accordingly, and with very little fear, she drove her elbow hard into Joseph's ribs and her heel into the horse's side. Just what she had intended even she was not quite sure, but Joseph, surprised and suddenly winded, released his hold upon the reins and fell backwards out of the saddle, his pistol exploding as he did so. The horse had sprung forward in considerable alarm, and now, with the sound of a pistol discharging itself once more in her vicinity, bolted. For a second Genevieve clung desperately to her mane, but not only did she have no hold upon the reins, she did not sit in the saddle, and survived on horseback for no more than a moment. She had a vision of trees whirling strangely about her and then blackness descended.

CHAPTER
TWELVE

GENEVIEVE awoke, and all was silent. She lay in bed, a large, soft bed, and covers had been carefully pulled to her chin. Around her were hangings that seemed vaguely familiar. The whole atmosphere, in fact, was one she knew she ought to recollect. She sat up, and cautiously parted one curtain.

She was in a wide, high room, its ceiling ornate, its long windows hung with curtains to match those about the bed. Sun streamed through onto a thick, cream-coloured carpet, and through the window she could see the branches of some tall, leafless tree. There was the sound of bird-song. A wrap that was not hers lay across the chair at her side. She reached out and pulled it around her shoulders, and then set bare feet to the floor. Standing at the window she could see now across a wide park, its trees stark still, but the ground beneath splashed purple with crocus. Beyond the trees was a glint of water; she could now hear the distant harsh call of a heron. Movement beneath her attracted her eye downwards. A carriage had drawn up before what must be the front door, and as she watched a tall gaunt figure she knew too well descended to the gravel and shook out her skirts.

Recollection came in a rush. She must be at Dearing, it was the only explanation. Somehow Robert had res-

cued her and she was back in his home again, after
having contrived to escape. She thought rapidly, and
then ran to the dressing-room in search of her clothes.
They were all there, plus quite a number that she did not
recognise that must have been bought for her. She felt a
curious lurch in her stomach as she fingered the fine stuff
and wondered if Robert had chosen them himself, and if
so how he had known her size. But such thoughts were
idle and without point. Resolutely she selected one of
her own dresses and began divesting herself of her
nightgown.

She took nothing with her. Not stopping to wonder
how she would fare with not the slightest particle of
luggage, or even how such a destitute young lady travelling alone must appear, she flung her pelisse about her
shoulders and cautiously opened the door. The passage,
for the moment at least, was deserted, but she knew it
could not be long before Miss Pinkerton was brought
upstairs. She recognised where she was and knew that if
she could only gain the far end of this passage she would
find a spiral stairway that led to the stable-yard, a device
that made it unnecessary for muddied riders to traverse
the entire house before reaching their rooms. No doubt
there could be grooms in the yard; people would be
attending to the team that had brought Miss Pinkerton,
but she did not doubt her ability to avoid them. In a
moment she had reached the ground floor and was
peering into the yard. It must be late afternoon, she
decided. There was that golden quality about the sun as
it streamed through the yard that comes only towards
sunset, and there was, besides, quite a chill in the air.
She wondered for a moment if she would have been wise
to have brought her sables, and then dismissed the idea.
Such a policy would almost certainly have drawn the

meanest pickpocket in her direction. There were two men in the yard, but neither was looking towards the door. Miss Pinkerton's team had already been led away and these two were engrossed in some earnest discussion that left them no time for looking about. Genevieve caught up her skirts and began crossing the yard.

She had gone barely ten steps when she heard a horse approaching. A visitor, perhaps? She would need to brave him, then, for the rider was coming straight for the stables. She took a few more steps and then she could see him, trotting gently up the finely gravelled drive. For a moment she stood frozen, and then she raised her chin a little and walked on. It was only when he came almost abreast of her that she realised it was her husband.

There was no avoiding him now. However could she have been so foolish as not to recognise him? He had drawn his animal in and, as one of the grooms came running towards him, swung himself to the ground.

'I am sorry to be so late,' Sir Robert said easily, surrendering the reins and taking her arm. 'I dare say you think me most dreadfully rude, but Jervis is really worried about the long field. I had thought to plant oats this year but he says it must lie fallow. But I'm boring you. Tell me, is Miss Pinkerton arrived? A carriage passed us while we were inspecting five-acre field.'

Genevieve found her voice sufficiently to say that she thought Miss Pinkerton had arrived, but she had not yet seen her.

'Ah. No doubt Mrs Trimble is taking care of her. She's an admirable housekeeper, Valentine I do hope you will find her satisfactory as I should be loath to part with her.'

'Oh yes!' Genevieve managed, succumbing to the pressure on her arm and moving forward.

'I'm so glad,' Sir Robert said, smiling down at her

particularly warmly. 'I wonder, will you go in without me? I am, as you see, sadly muddied, or I should accompany you. Perhaps you would bear with me a little longer, and await me in the blue drawing-room? There is something I particularly wish to say to you before Miss Pinkerton comes down. Promise me you'll wait for me there. Promise me, Valentine!'

Genevieve hesitated, and then nodded. What else could she have done, after all? If only he had not come just then! But there was nothing she could do. She would have to tell him everything. If only it could all be over before she saw Miss Pinkerton! She gained the door, and slipped inside.

The lackey in attendance there showed not the slightest surprise at his mistress's sudden appearance. His face expressionless he bowed, and moved to open the door to the blue drawing-room, towards which Genevieve had unconsciously been walking. Wordlessly he received Genevieve's pelisse and, with another bow, closed the door behind her. Genevieve, hardly aware of his actions, sat down. It was a great deal too bad, she decided, that she was obliged to go through the interview that would almost certainly follow, especially since she had been at such pains to avoid it. She tried to rehearse what she would say, but her brain seemed strangely woollen, and refused to function. For the first time she wondered how long she had lain unconscious in that bed, and whether this strange sensation in her head was the result of her fall. She had just come to the conclusion that it must be so when the door opened and her husband was at her side.

'I am so glad you waited for me,' he said easily, glancing briefly at her and then moving to look out of the window. 'I had wanted to be with you when you awoke.'

'Have—have I been unconscious for very long?' she managed at last, totally forgetting any pretence at an accent.

He smiled at her. 'Three days. You hit your head rather hard, I'm afraid, but the doctor assured me there was no lasting harm. However, I do not think you should be wandering about the stables quite yet.' He paused, searching in an inside pocket. 'Miss Pinkerton will be delighted to see you, Valentine,' he said, discovering his snuff-box finally and flicking it open. 'She was really quite distressed at your manner of leaving, and was so relieved when I was able to tell her you were really quite well.'

'Oh dear!' Genevieve said, not knowing quite where to look. It was going to be a great deal worse than she had envisaged.

'Perhaps,' Sir Robert suggested gently, 'it might have been better had you told her of your marriage. I fear the news came as quite a shock. Apparently,' he continued with a little smile, 'she had almost persuaded herself you were little more than a common thief. A snuff-box, or some such thing. Happily I was able to convince her that you were nothing of the sort. It was a great relief to her, you may be sure. I do not believe she found it easy to think such things of you.'

'Oh dear!' Genevieve exclaimed again. 'I have behaved very badly.'

'Well, I do think you have been a little thoughtless,' Robert conceded, carefully flicking a speck from his olive sleeve. 'And I do wish you could find it in your heart to trust us.' He smiled. 'Am I such an ogre, my love? Do you find the thought of confiding in me so utterly repulsive?'

He had moved from the window and now stood over

her, smiling so very kindly and with such understanding that her heart began behaving in a very strange manner indeed. Unable to speak, she shook her head.

'Then I wish you would do so!' Robert exclaimed, lifting his coat-tails and sitting at her side. 'Indeed, there are a great many things I should like to know, particularly why you had chosen to hire a carriage when a much better one had already been provided.'

Genevieve stared at him, but did not reply.

'Also,' Robert continued, 'why you had chosen such strange persons as your companions. One of them—a Mr Smith?—seemed to be under the impression that you were going to France with him, but I assured him he was mistaken.'

'Please,' Genevieve managed to say, 'I can't answer these questions now. My head—'

'My dear, I am very thoughtless. Pray forgive me. I shall call Mary at once. She will help you to your room.'

'Mary?' Genevieve's voice was barely audible, but Sir Robert, who had risen, turned back with a smile.

'Why yes. Do you not want her? She is in the servants' hall.'

'Here?'

Sir Robert nodded. 'Of course. She came back from London on her own, Valentine, and reached here before you did.'

'Oh.' Genevieve hung her head. 'I don't know what to say. Whatever must you think of me?'

The last was a choking note, and Sir Robert, his expression concerned, sat down again and took her agitated hands in a firm grip, 'If only you would trust me,' he said, trying without success to look into her face. 'I assure you, there is nothing you can tell me that would make me think the worse of you, or even love you any less than I do now.'

Genevieve raised her head, and for a moment stared into her husband's face. Then, with a strange choking sound, the tears that had been withheld for so long finally erupted. She dragged one hand from Sir Robert's grasp and covered her eyes. 'Pray do not! You do not know what I would tell you!'

Sir Robert sighed. It would seem as though he would have to admit it to her after all. 'I wish you would tell me what is troubling you,' he said, making one last effort.

With an effort Genevieve removed her hand from her eyes and looked at her husband. 'I am not what you think me,' she said.

Sir Robert smiled and kissed the fingers of the hand he yet held. 'Are you not?' he said gently.

'No. Have you not noticed? My accent?' He was being strangely obtuse, she thought.

'Your accent?' For a moment Sir Robert frowned. Then he said, 'Oh, your French accent? You should not worry about that, you know. I like you just as well without it.'

'I am not French!' Genevieve cried, wondering what she had to do to make this man understand.

'I know.'

'You know? How can you know?'

Sir Robert smiled, and leaned back against the chair. 'The very first night you were here, remember, I was very late for dinner. You were charming enough to make no comment about it, even though it was quite unforgivable. However, I had been most interestingly occupied. Your maid, my dear, your Mary, had decided to tell me the most fascinating story, a story about a young girl, the daughter of an Englishman and a French lady, who had come to England some five years ago after they had both perished, in a fire I believe. She had with her her young brother, barely fifteen at the time, and they were to live with an aunt in—' he frowned—'Harrogate? Yes, Harrogate. Unfortunately the week before their arrival this aunt also had perished, and the pair were left with very little more than they carried with them. They would have gone to the Parish, but the young woman, who had heard of such institutions from her English father, was determined that this should not occur. Accordingly, with the assistance of her faithful maid, she set about earning a living for herself, and her young brother.' He paused, and smiled at Genevieve's horror-struck face. 'The morals of her subsequent conduct do not concern us. It is enough to say she managed well enough, arriving finally at a mansion in Bedfordshire, the home of one Claudius Lyle.'

'You know everything.'

Sir Robert smiled. 'I know a great deal. Only you can tell me if I know everything.'

She did not heed him. 'Why did you not tell me? Why did you let me carry on with such a charade?' She glared at him for a moment or two, her bosom heaving with indignation, and then her eyes narrowed. 'Sir Robert, you talk of your great-uncle, Claudius Lyle. How long have you known about me?'

For a second Sir Robert did not answer, and the smile faded from his face. It was replaced by a grave look. 'My dearest child, you are the only thing in the world that matters to me. Can't you believe that?'

'You knew!' The words were a pained cry. 'From the first moment we met you knew who I was! *You knew*!' Shame and indignation battled for supremacy. He had known all the time what she was trying to do, which was unpardonable in him, but since he did know, how could she possibly hope for any rekindling of that love he had once borne her? Or had he? If not, why had he married her, knowing everything as he did? Pained and confused, her words very muffled, and then, 'Whatever must you think of me?'

'I consider you to be a little fool,' Sir Robert said, possessing himself of those agitated hands and holding them firmly. 'And I think besides that if you do not forget your previous life and settle down to being Lady Lyle of Dearing you will find yourself in a very sorry state. Besides which,' he added, raising her hands to his lips and kissing them, 'I have no intention of letting you go.'

'But this is ridiculous!' Genevieve protested, trying half-heartedly to free her hands. 'How can you possibly wish me to remain your wife when I deceived you so very dreadfully?'

'But you did not,' Sir Robert pointed out. 'I knew from the first what you were about, and indeed, if any blame is to be attached, it should be to me for I set myself very much in your way.'

Genevieve stared at him. 'You did?'

He nodded. 'I have to admit, my dearest girl, that I intended from the first being your next target, and indeed, for quite some time I congratulated myself on the success of my little plan. Unfortunately I had not taken into account the fact that I would become hopelessly in love with you within a very short space of time. In fact, for quite a while I was at a loss how to bring the thing to a satisfactory conclusion.'

'You were?'

He nodded again. 'When I realised that you were only going to marry me because you needed the money for your brother I felt quite desolate. If Mary had not decided to confide in me I dare say you would have been in France by now.'

Genevieve did not speak. It seemed, ridiculous though it was, as if Sir Robert did not care who she was, or what she had done, but it was almost too good to be true and she raised anxious eyes to his face. 'Sir Robert,' she said, 'do you really understand what I have been doing these last five years? Your old uncle was not the first. There were—quite a few others.'

'I know about that too. Mary told me. And you may rest easy, for I have sent them all bankers' drafts for the sums you—er borrowed. In your name, or I should say names, my dear.'

'You did? All—three of them?'

'All five of them, my love, including my unfortunate Uncle Claudius.'

'Oh.' Genevieve was silenced again.

'And that brings us to the matter of your young brother.'

'Oh yes. George.'

She sounded so despondent that Sir Robert was moved to laugh. 'My dear, only last week he was the summit of your concerns! According to Mary you could talk of nothing other than your poor George and how you had let him down.'

'I know. It's quite true. Only, you see, while I was in that awful wood with your brother I realised that George would probably do a great deal better for himself than I ever could, and resolved, if I should survive, never to worry about him again.'

'I am overjoyed to hear it. But I should tell you, just in case you should take it into your head to become anxious again, that he is, by this time, safely in France, and that a surgeon attended him before he left, to ensure his safe arrival in that country. So you may rest easy.'

'Thank you,' Genevieve said dolefully.

'You may like to know, also,' Robert continued with a wry smile, 'just what befell my own brother.'

'Your brother? Oh yes, your brother! Do tell me. I trust you did not let him go for I am sure he meant to kill us both, which is really a great deal too bad.'

'It is indeed,' Sir Robert agreed, controlling his lip with an effort. 'So I did not let him escape entirely. He took a bullet, you know, in the shoulder. That was your doing, I believe. He certainly had a great many unkind things to say about you.'

'Did he? Well, I can't be sorry he was wounded, though I suppose one ought not to wish him dead.'

'No, and he is not. In fact, he has gone to France with George, where I trust they might deal extremely together. Indeed, I hope they do!'

Genevieve looked up at him, and a chuckle escaped her. 'Oh yes, I hope so, indeed. I only wish I might be there to see it.'

'That I shall not permit,' Sir Robert answered firmly. 'From now on you are to comfort yourself as befits the new Lady Lyle, which means, I am afraid, no more French accents.'

'It does?' Genevieve seemed a little doubtful. 'Will people not think it strange?'

'I dare say they will, but you shall contrive to live it down, my dear, and when they see that I have no intention of discussing it with them the matter will cease to be a miracle. I dare say it will be quite forgotten in a decade or two.'

'A decade!' Genevieve echoed, horror-struck. 'Indeed, Sir Robert, I do not think I can wait that long.

Would it not be better for me to continue with the accent, and just gradually acquire an English one?'

Sir Robert smiled. 'That is exactly what you will do, my love. By the time we appear in Town again, which will be, I think, not for a month or two, your command of the English language will have improved so markedly that no one who did not know will guess you are not English. And those who do will merely marvel at your brilliance.'

Genevieve risked a little smile. 'Do you really think so?'

'I am sure so,' he answered, putting an arm about her shoulders and pulling her close.

'I am glad,' she confided into his coat, 'for you must know, Sir Robert, that I really wished for nothing more than to be your wife.'

'I do know,' Sir Robert assured her, 'but if we are to continue this charade I believe you must stop calling me Sir Robert.'

She raised her head and smiled shyly up at him. 'Do you know, I shall find that very difficult.'

'I agree that it will be one of the harder parts of your new life, but to allay suspicion I am afraid it is totally necessary.'

'Totally?'

He nodded grimly, 'So I suggest you try it at once.'

'Very well—Robert!'

Sir Robert felt moved to smile, to which his bride responded so charmingly that he was obliged to take her into his arms and kiss her soundly.